THE WATER CURE

Also by PERCIVAL EVERETT

Wounded

Damned If I Do

American Desert

*A History of the African–American People (Proposed)
by Strom Thurmond
As Told to Percival Everett and James Kincaid*

Erasure

Glyph

Frenzy

Watershed

Big Picture

The Body of Martin Aguilera

God's Country

For Her Dark Skin

Zulus

The Weather and the Women Treat Me Fair

Cutting Lisa

Walk Me to the Distance

Suder

The One That Got Away

THE WATER CURE

Percival Everett

GRAYWOLF PRESS
Saint Paul, Minnesota

Publication of this volume is made possible in part by a grant provided by the Minnesota State Arts Board, through an appropriation by the Minnesota State Legislature; a grant from the Wells Fargo Foundation Minnesota; and a grant from the National Endowment for the Arts, which believes that a great nation deserves great art. Significant support has also been provided by the Bush Foundation; Target; the McKnight Foundation; and other generous contributions from foundations, corporations, and individuals. To these organizations and individuals we offer our heartfelt thanks.

Published by Graywolf Press
2402 University Avenue, Suite 203
Saint Paul, Minnesota 55114
All rights reserved.

www.graywolfpress.org

Published in the United States of America

ISBN 978-1-55597-476-3

2 4 6 8 9 7 5 3 1
First Graywolf Printing, 2007

Library of Congress Control Number: 2007924763

Cover design: www.VetoDesignUSA.com

Cover art: iStockphoto

For DANZY,
with all my love

The truth rests with God
and a little bit with me.
            —Yiddish proverb

. . . so we induce

and

find

the arduous nowhere.

***

These pages are my undertaking. I am guilty not because of my actions, to which I freely admit, but for my accession, admission, confession that I executed these actions with not only deliberation and premeditation but with zeal and paroxysm and purpose, above all else purpose, that I clearly articulate without apology or qualification, and so I find myself merely a sign, a clear sign, and like any sign I am indifferent to the nature of the thing that I designate or, for lack of a better word, signify, while scratching at the dried blood beneath my nails, my voice rough and hoarse from disuse, for no matter how articulate my confession, it takes few words to utter it, the truth always requiring fewer words, and generally smaller words, than lies and half-truths, and they are never called half-lies, and this is instructive, the way so many things are *instructive*, and it all comes back to that indifference to the marked thing, the way nouns and names behave badly and play loose with meaning, the way language resists the tightening of screws and the sketching of schema and the way the angle of incidence complements the angle of reflection: the whole mess of language yearning for a decent visual metaphor to connect it with the world toward which it is so indifferent. The true answer to your question is shorter than the lie. Did you? I did.

***

A dead face is no face at all, at all no face, no face it is not cold, not plastic, no longer flesh, all dream, all thought, it is all too human and animal and human and even expressive, but it is no face at all and one can hold a living face in one's hands, but a dead face sifts through fingers, leaks, drips, no face, a living face gives back even when sleeping even when unconscious, but a dead face absorbs one's gaze, stretches that search for connection to infinity, the familiar functions of connection, addition, subtraction, multiplication, and division do not work for dead faces, as they do not work as arithmetical procedures for infinite decimals, a dead face, like an infinite decimal, corresponds to nothing in the real world, a dead face is a concept, and so one cannot hold it in one's hands, and so I hold my daughter's living face, her once-living face, that face that I loved and, with my then-wife, made, as a reality in my mind, resisting the common, persisting, unhelpful belief that memories are every time newly constructed, cultivated, harvested, no face at all my daughter's sweet sweet face is a real living thing inside me, abstract and real, never gone so never in need of reconstructing and somewhere there is a thing in this world, my world, the only world that is her sweet dead face, no face at all, perhaps a symbol, a sign, a directional beacon, a denoting or connoting marker but no face at all.

***

Ce n'est que jeu de mots, qu'affectation pure.

***

"Hey, did you hear the one about the . . ."

***

For me, salvation is not a place of comfort, however good that place might feel, but a place of safety, contentment, a place, whether physical, emotional, or intellectual, that is free of external voices and a couple of internal ones as well. Salvation, it turns out, is a couple of map-folds away from serenity. Salvation might keep you alive, but it won't make you happy about it.

I used to find serenity in the face of my daughter, but that state went missing, as did she, turned up missing, as it was put, as if a person, a life, an idea can be discovered by the realization of its absence. Lane was eleven years old, a small eleven, when she was abducted and only two days older when her small body was found with all her life having turned up missing. She had been too young to truly imagine death, too young to have understood enough of life to cherish it, but old enough to have taught me to do so, the lesson having been given with no fanfare, bells, singing, but quietly and, so, peculiarly, in a jarring fashion, like a self-slap to the forehead, as if to say, oh yeah, that's why we're here. Now, it is as if I have turned around to find a chalkboard erased of all that matters, the only remaining marks somehow indicating the date.

Lane had been standing in the front yard of her mother's house, just as she had a thousand times. There had no doubt been a light, maybe cool breeze, and perhaps a cloud had drifted in front of the sun. Charlotte had seen the child there, leaning on her bicycle, and just minutes later, the bicycle was there alone, laid on the grass between the uneven sidewalk and the street, that strip of land which could have belonged to the city or to Charlotte, a place where the child had never laid her bicycle before. Twenty minutes passed, then another twenty minutes, then another of Charlotte driving slowly, with increasing panic, through her neighborhood. She called me from her driveway, her panic working its way into numbness that finally led to the question, "What do I do?"

"Call the police," I said.

"The police?"

"I'll be right there."

I did not close my files. I grabbed my keys from my desk, left my wallet and license on the kitchen table, and took the elevator down to my car. I can still feel that haunting, hollow sensation, an ice lance at the back of my stomach, as if I had forgotten to eat, the cavity of my gut quiet and hard. There was a police cruiser in the drive when I pulled up. Charlotte was going over it all again: white sneakers with red stripes, light blue jeans, a darker blue T-shirt, a blue hooded sweatshirt— "Blue is her favorite color," she offered nervously—brown skin, a head full of wild dark hair.

Charlotte and I had not been close for several years, despite our belief and vocal claim that our split had been amicable, but the child was ours and when she saw me, she embraced me and I hugged her back. The physical reconnection punctuated the gravity of the situation. The fear had to find some release, and it became an irritation with the policemen who were standing in the driveway instead of scouring the streets.

"Why aren't you out looking?" is what Charlotte said.

"We are, ma'am," said a sturdy policeman, and we apparently believed him.

No one had seen anything. At least they had seen nothing that made them think to remember it. No strange cars, no strange vans, no strange or odd-looking men. And so a long-standing philosophical question was answered for me: if your child screams in the forest and there is no one around to hear, does she make a sound? It turns out that she does not.

The police canvassed the darkening neighborhood twice

and then again. There was no so-called Amber Alert because there was no car description to release to the public. Charlotte went back into her house, I believed, to search it for the thousandth time, and I drove over the same pavement until I became the strange and suspicious car that residents might recall.

I returned to Charlotte's house that night to find her being comforted by her boyfriend, a nice enough fellow who was in way over his head now. He stood there while fear and familiarity combined to bring Charlotte and me close once again. And yet, not really, as none of our concern, rightly, ever became for the fear and pain of the other. We wanted only our daughter. More precisely, to emphasize the division, she wanted her daughter, and I wanted mine. I had to give Buck or Chuck or whatever-his-name-was credit because he hung in there, fetching water and peering out the window and at the idle telephone. He fell asleep in a stuffed chair while Charlotte drank pot after pot of tea and I paced. The next day came with far too clear a morning. Charlotte peed with the door open and watched the phone. The police came early to tell us that they had no reason to be there so early and so they left and the day stretched out as a tedious exercise of clock watching. The boyfriend and I drove our separate cars in widening circles of desperation and though he was in another place altogether, I decided that I liked him and hoped Charlotte would be happy with him and then realized that all my thinking was an act of self-preservative distraction.

Early the next morning, a detective, a woman, came to Charlotte's door, and we all saw this as a bad sign and in fact it was, as the news she delivered was that a young girl matching Lane's description had been found in a ravine beside a park by two boys and their dog. She had gone into so much detail, it seemed to me, about the park that led to a ditch that fed into a concrete drainage canal, and the boys, aged nine and ten, not brothers, but across-the-street neighbors, that I found myself asking, without knowing why or even that I was asking, "What kind of dog was it?"

* * *

I come from a nation of stupid fucks and by association, at least, if not genetic inevitability, a sobering and sickening thought, I must be a stupid fuck as well. The stupid fucks in my country elected a king stupid fuck, and he ruled with stupid fuck glory and majesty, a stupid fuck for the ages, who in a more fair time might have been successful as the man who follows behind the circus parade with a shovel, but probably not. The stupid fuck was elected by stupid fucks and supported by stupid fucks and even occasionally fell out of favor with stupid fucks, but stupid fucks, being stupid fucks, either forgot or forgave and again loved the king stupid fuck who loved war and money and butchering the language while chewing at the inside of his cheek, polluting the air with slogans like, *If you can't find your enemy, create one* and *When in doubt, fear and hate*, though my favorite unused one is *It's Us against Them, too bad We're not all Us*. But I too am a stupid fuck, if for no other reason than for calling you a stupid fuck and expecting you to read on and for writing this bit to open this bigger bit that might or might not have anything to do with my entire project here, if indeed it is a project, a book, a mission, a work, a journal, or graffiti. Yes, graffiti, that is what this is, my messages scribbled across boxcars and bridges and the sheet-metal fences encircling scrap yards.

* * *

As if anything matters.

* * *

It is always a matter of framing, of framing matter. Of paintings, whether they are framed or not, whether the frame wears the work, or whether the frame is an essential part of some artistic expression, who frames and why, when, and for whom. Is the frame a work of art apart from the framed, and if so, is it a frame at all, and what docs it mean to consider that they, the frame and the framed, work together or against each other? Is the frame a decision or an accident? Can there be a break in the frame? Is a frame with a break a frame at all? And after all a frame is just a box, and a box is just a container, but what a container does, in addition to *containing,* if it ever does that at all, marking what is inside, is mark what is outside. A box, a frame, a container, one's skin not so much surround a thing, but close out a world that is not surrounded.

Life, framed as it is by birth on one end and death on the other (granted, not a sophisticated idea, or a new one for that matter), is not the frame, nor is it the edges of the frame, and it is not large and grand gestures within the frame, but rather life consists in small, idle, nugatory gestures, small like eating lunch, walking to the mailbox, cleaning out the car's trunk, remembering where you parked, forgetting to kiss your daughter good night. Life is not great deeds, but little, almost insignificant sneezes of time, Lilliputian hiccups of things we might or might not recall, might or might not choose to recall. Need I too to to find my way way back to the way wry rhythm rinsed rhythm that is my heartbeatskipbeat any anymore? It is always eternally invariably a matter of framing, of framing matter and oh, with just a slip of a letter, a dyslexic pratfall framing becomes farming, and that's a whole other kettle of fish.

***

And so this begins, as all things must begin, at the beginning and with a conjunction.

A pause here as I muddle through the muddle. Does it all begin with a definite article? Do we back up in time forever? If we figure out what follows the THE in the first sentence, then do we have god? Or is god the THE, the definite article, a definite article *not being interchangeable with* the real thing? *If the stuff of what we call the universe goes backward infinitely (the big bang aside as it is only a bout of question begging), then what of infinity itself? Is infinity a necessary truth or a necessary construction? All of this when all we want is to sail around on the watery part of the world. As you can see, this is my substitute for pistol and ball. And yet the sea, all seas, the ocean of air above me will roll on like it did five thousand years ago, like it will five thousand years from now.*

Back to our regularly scheduled program:

All things in the world (where else?) are necessarily attached to some other thing or things in the world that in turn necessarily attach to other things and so on, the contingent or conditional attachments being necessary and ineludible features. Contingency itself, therefore, is necessary, if for no other reason than it allows the notion of necessity to make sense. There's a place for everyone and everyone in her or his place and so I am here (a rather vague and iffy concept or designation at best), attached to the wall or nailed to the floor, moving

14

through this door or leaping out that window, stumbling down this road or trotting right up the old alley, attaching myself spatially or psychically or narratively to some other person, place, thing, thought, or even pain (perhaps the only thing that is truly shared by all of us). Places change. Feelings are immutable, so we are instructed (by those who instruct), but every emotion has a precise (if plastic) story, a history, an apologue, and therefore is attached to this thing we call a world and cannot exist without it. Blah, blah, blah. Call me Ishmael.

***

Entering here, in the middle, like a Dedekind blade splitting a line, in this particular frame or section of this frame, left to *remar contra a mar,* you are at a disadvantage. But who cares? One is easily caught up, as if that is the point, to be caught up, to know where we are in the story, to understand a context, to be in the know.

Regard:
The extent of things is always just that and that only, and the limits of any piece are like the arbitrarily drawn boundaries of a nation or a borderline defined by a river, the former subject to alteration by the whim of aggressive, greedy, and small men, and the latter to the somewhat less impetuous decisions of nature. My name is in fact Ishmael. Ishmael Kidder.

***

There is a vermilion flycatcher on a skinny branch of a stunted live oak not four feet from me. The flycatchers on this mountain almost never let me get so close. I used to put out feeders, but the seeds and suet attracted rodents and skunks. I decided to let the garden alone be enough meal for the birds, but this muted version of her fire-headed male counterpart is not here for seed or suet. *Pyrocephalus rubinus,* a tyrant flycatcher, tyrannide, unusual up here on this dry-ass mountain. There is no stream here. She pops up and efficiently hawks an insect from the thin air every few minutes, then lights back onto her perch and watches me, studies me through her dark mask. I stare at her through mine.

***

As a oneder-loving and wonder-see king sort, I will exhighbit esnuff off myshelf, my deep sadnest asidle, my disillusionmantle acider, my fear and lax thereof asighed, my asides aslide, to yiell a bravf picture of the main I yam, my preverse colloudiness aside. And so I weight, my bird, my spiright, my sorehorse, my slights havink flown. I leak aboot and keep yondering when my Pinel or Tuke might enthere and caste oft these chains. Nyet, I cuncider this life a prism, meself mhad, tall this in spite of my comforit, sew-called, exstream combfort that costs me so much discomfjord and then gilt for feeling bad abutt feeling good and one tit goes untilt the doctorn enters the asshighlum.

***

Fragments. Frag-ments. Frags. Fr. m ents. This work is not fragmented;
    it is fragments.

So, all sections are fragments, except for this one because it lives here, in this spot, among the fragments, and has a specified job concerning those fragments surrounding it. A fragment? Connective tissue? The story itself?

Oh, the story itself, that ever-thickening center.

And there is some debt, death, dumb-de-dee-do death be debt and here is grammar for grammar's sake and here is a drink to toast the dumb-do-day man who

breaks and brittles and bobs his head as if the music meant something, means something, meats something, yes meats, meets something, meets someone at the bottom of the glass we raise to toast the dumb-dare-dial the number of the nearest kin

***

The call, rather the asomatous, disembodied voice placing the call informed me that the individual (that was how he called him, the individual) had been caught, captured, apprehended, snagged, that the criminal, the scoundrel, the transgressor had been secured, his word, secured, that the murderer was in custody, behind bars, off the streets. Something about DNA. Something about possible circumstantial evidence. None of it rang clearly. None of it rang as truth. None of it rang in any intelligible way, or rang at all for that matter. A dead bell. A bell in a vacuum. The dead are still dead. No matter who lives or dies, the dead remain dead. That is all the dead have to do, all that is required of them, to stay that way.

***

We can count forever. That is infinity, so to speak. But we do not have names for most of the numbers in the world of infinity. This is one million: 1,000,000.

What is this called? 1,000,000,000,000,000,000,000,
000,000,000,000,000,001.

We do not have infinite words. But we could. If we wanted to we could. If we wanted to. Is there a name for this want? If we want one. We can talk forever.

And we will.

But what is the name of this desire? If I find a need to refer to it, what shall I call it? Hydrophobia is the fear of water. Francophilia is the love of things French. What is the name of my desire for infinite words? And, mind you, that is not the same as infinite language.

We certainly can have a name for it, this desire for infinite words, if we want one.

We can name it if we choose.

And if we don't? Does the desire exist?

The name of this desire for infinite words is *love*. But you cannot have the desire unless you love infinitely.

***

If there ever is an end, only if there is an end, when there is an end, then and only then, after all else and at the end, will we tally up the score and count the dead. Well, you can count, if you like.

***

A puzzle:

A man is standing on the bank of a wide river. With him are a monster, a child, and a bag of chocolates. He must get all three to the other side, but his boat is so small that he can take only one across at a time. He could not ever leave the monster with the child for it would eat her, and he could not leave the child with the chocolates for she would eat them. The monster hates chocolates and would never touch them. How does the man get all three across?

***

Here is a picture of my daughter:

***

The fragments of Heraclitus, just over a hundred, are important, if I may make that claim, in a way, simply because they are fragments. Some wonder whether the fragments come from one large work or from many works, whether Heraclitus had some literary scheme or whether he was, well, like me. Like his peers (and everyone else, it seems), he is credited with having written a book titled *On Nature*. I come to this as an escape (not quite the same as an escapee), this philosophy, this dabbling, a mere distraction. It is my therapy, though I'm not sure what therapy is supposed to do for me.

Heraclitus's fragments tend to be gnomic, aphoristic, and oracular, sometimes contradictory, often mercurial, and to my glee (an archaic word, an archaic concept, at least for me), full of metaphors and even puns.

The Sibyl with raving mouth utters, solemn, unadorned, unlovely words, and reaches over a thousand years with her voice, thanks to the god in her. The lord whose oracle is a Delphic neither utters nor hides his meaning, but shows it by sign.

***

***

Tap tap tap on your forehead, friend. Tap tap tap on your brim-less briny brain. Monologues are always about the world. Re-member that—rip rip rip. Think of the repetitions as crumbs left on the trail, your way out. Follow the pains, follow the tap tap tap on your face. Follow the ripping of the tape. Make them familiar. Make them yours. Learn the taste of the adhesive.

***

Loss the loss of a person or a thing loved no matter the circumstances wipes irony from the corners of our mouths but irony
is tenacious hardly ironic some words can just hang in the air
without context without mission loss of a child and sentences
beg for structure or do we, sounding almost the same but far
from the same, saying saying consider this war, consider this
conquest this house hours in this breathing house, sticky blood
and how many priests it takes to screw in a lightbulb or screw
at all for that matter

    And sentences beg for question marks and periods as lives
beg for anything as religion begs for suckers and citizens beg
for certainties and governments beg for forgiveness like mo-
lesters and murderers lining sofas benches walls with fingers
crossed behind their backs stepped on a crack like when we
were children breaking backs and meanness was just a way to
be and feel bad about it later and when we did we were made
all right okay all better by the knowledge that we were merely
children little tikes innocents but when grown up what do we
have a laundry list of excuses knuckles red from scuffling veins
bloated with blood and you my friend my friend bound to be a
problem a problem bound once a child and too bad you're not
one now you could get a pass maybe maybe

    tug tug

    Is this too tight?

***

To pierce the thyme, instood of writhing, meye being a wrider,
I half talken to this, whatnever this tis, seven wiff this stein

warkning. This is allways marely thistle and somefines this and that, but filenally this. This is the weigh we wash our cloaves. This is the way. This well never due.

***

It is considered a chronic, progressive illness, *progressive* offering wonderful mis- or missed readings, and supposedly there is no cure. If I never in life do it (drink, booze, partake, imbibe) again, if you allow that phrasing and even if you don't, then who is to say that I was not cured and if I do, in life, do it again, then who is to say that I was not cured and then merely re-infected. Is it always the old cancer awaiting its opportunity to reappear? Can't there be a new cancer, even if it affects the same organ? But then perhaps I was not ill at all, but simply stupid, dumber than most, weak-willed, indulgent, lazy. Choice is an interesting thing in that it is always what it is, choice; tautologies are not to be argued with, but that is a matter for debate. There is a difference between "I cannot run another yard" and "I will not run another yard." And the difference is not because *cannot* is not the same as *will not*. It is because the *I's* are different.

Most animals, wild or not, react to predator behavior in one of two ways, the "illness" (oh, but isn't that a sad move on my part, to not only call my weakness an illness, but to mark it with quotation marks, thus assuring that it will be read as an illness and as an admission of my self-knowledge, my self-aware acceptance of its problematic status as an "illness") perhaps exhibiting predatory (and then give the problematized disease agency? How low can I sink?) tendencies—perhaps.

***

Fighting. Running. Fleeing. Prey animals will turn and fight when trapped, but they prefer to run. "Prefer" here is problematic as it suggests a thought process I am not prepared to defend. Nonetheless, running might have been my *preferred* "preferred" response.

It has always been my belief that delay is highly preferable to error. But my country has instructed me differently. I have come to love my country for this example, for this license, for this vanity.

But still, if there is a god and if that god is a just god, then I tremble for my country.

***

What I know of Thales comes from Aristotle, and so it is not a lot, what I know. Aristotle speaks of Thales in the *Metaphysics* and *De Anima*. With a bit of condescension, an attitude he was wont to adopt, Aristotle identifies Thales as "the founder of *this* kind of philosophy." According to Aristotle, Thales says, "that the principle is water [and therefore declared the earth to be on water], perhaps taking the supposition from the fact that the nutriment of all things is moist, that from which they come to be the principle of things." And then, as if fed up or drowned by Thales, Aristotle snaps, "Thales at any rate is said to have explained the principles and origins of things in this way." I love the "at any rate." From what A says in the two books, though he does mention him in other places, *De Caelo*, for example, Thales's story is essentially this:

> Water is the essence of all things.
> All things have soul in them
> The all is divine.

But, but, but, and I mean that clearly, surely, and in every conditional sense of the word, I have and do live comfortably in
this life, am able to write novels (romance though they be) for
a living, able to drink alcohol to excess much of my days and
privileged enough to occasionally correct that particular social,
moral, or medical malfunction or at least be forgiven for it by
those around me (perhaps this is the real addiction). Luckily,
I am wealthy. Forgiveness in this culture requires money, and
if not money then wealth, a distinction that might not be clear
but is true enough. All of this embarrasses me greatly, but to
no great effect. I never meant to live this long.

The extent of things is always just that, and the limits of
any piece of fiction are like the ubiquitous musings of Zeno,
dismissible yet true, superficially simple but persistently gnawing and troubling, a thorn in the side of any traveler. I simply
am of course who I am, Ishmael Kidder, but I am better known
as Estelle Gilliam, the romance novelist. No one knows that I
am Estelle Gilliam, not around here. My ex-wife knows, but
she lives far away in another life on that other planet, with
a separate grief. The local constable knows; I was forced to
confess my identity to forestall his presumption that I was, in
his words, "a drug-runnin' bastard dog son of a bitch," since
he believed that anyone with no visible means of support must
be a drug dealer. Unfortunately, he is not alone in that belief, as everyone in Taos, New Mexico, shares it. So, I am the
resident drug dealer, forced to turn away those who would buy
contraband from me and subject to the ridiculing stares of all
the rest, including the actual drug dealers who are certain I'm
stealing their business with the protection of the sheriff.

The one other person who knows who I am and am not

is my agent, a lovely person, extremely thin, shockingly so, with an equine face, pretty in her way, but apparently in no one else's. I know she is sick and she knows she is sick, but still she wastes away with the bony body, approaching limits of thinness that few know. I do not have a telephone, so her calls to me here on the mountain amount to her showing up. That I have no phone upsets everyone. That I hate the incessant ringing is not, I am told, a satisfactory reason. That I don't want to call anyone or be called by anyone is unintelligible to everyone else. That I would not answer if I had a phone falls on deaf ears, an irony I love.

Sally Lovely, that is my agent's name, is coming to find out why Estelle Gilliam has not delivered her new novel. Sally gets paid if and when I get paid and so she makes sure I'm paid and paid well. She's told me on many occasions that 15 percent of not much is even less. I have told her that her name is far better for the romance business than Estelle Gilliam.

But if this rings like story and I say to hell with story, with plot, and with trying to suggest that I am making any kind of statement about any kind of thing, art included. Art is tied up down in my basement and will never again see the sun, will never smell a flower again, with never feel rain, hear the wind, touch a puppy or a child.

* * *

I once watched a little girl, head framed with wild dark hair, on a big round blue like the dark sea trampoline. She did no tricks, no flips, no tucks or splits, but jumped up and down and up on the taut and blue surface, like midnight water stretched tight. Her smile and dark eyes grew wider with each strike of her little feet against the worried fabric as her little self bounced higher and higher still, becoming smaller at the peaks of her flights, the blue of forever her backdrop, and a blur all the rest of the way, higher, and her singing sounds, her lilting sounds—joy? Animal cries?

"Okay, that's enough, sweetie. Daddy has to go inside for a while."

"Can I keep doing this?"

"No, you can't be on this alone. You need me here to spot you."

"So, stay and spot me."

"Daddy has to go inside. Come on down."

"Just three more."

"No, now."

"Please? Three more."

"Okay, three more."

"On the third one, I'm going to touch the sun. Then we can go inside."

"Don't burn yourself."

"Burn myself?"

"On the sun. The sun is hot."

"Is the sun fire?"

"The sun is nothing but fire."

* * *

***

Nouns names, names nouns. A noun might be a name of that thing, but a proper name is not the name of that thing, but a name. My friend Peetles is a dog, so a dog is what she is and Peetles is what she is called. She is not a Peetles. She is Peetles. Likewise, she is not dog, but she is a dog. Unless of course I meet someone with a dog named Peetles, in which case I might say, "How odd, I have a Peetles, too." However, imagine that Peetles, my beautiful pet, has such a personality that all remark upon her. When guests come over, she tears around, running in circles, sliding across floors and all in a good-natured way. She is legendary. Imagine, but of course it will never happen, that Peetles passes on. I get a new dog, and I name her Pumpkin. When the guests arrive, she tears all about the house, and a friend says, "She's a real Peetles, isn't she." Nouns names verbs.

***

It is a bad silence or a density of feelings or perhaps a collapse of sensations altogether. It is not a matter of materialism. We simply seek some basis of exteriority, if you'll allow me such a word—and even if you won't, as I said before. The bad silences swim in glasses that are refilled, were refilled (mixed metaphors are a wonder). The bad silence, the bad silence——the bad   silence. There is no romance in the bad silences, and there is certainly no sound, nothing sound. In that absence, may I suggest that there resides the essence of art, the movement from sound, from language, to the ineffable, trying to make clear the obscurity of what is basic to all understanding. Art is the bad silence.

***

This is how I looked one morning, the morning that I realized that mornings were only mornings, merely mornings, and not the beginnings of days or of anything else for that matter. This is how I looked when my final recall became a final recall, and all that I recalled was finally final. This is how I looked when I was death warmed over, chilling on ice, slipping on the ice, iced over like a windshield on a freezing morning, but no mornings are freezing anymore, are they? Mornings are just mornings are just mornings are just what they are. And this is what I looked like when I realized that.

***

If I may, I will offer up again the metaphysical distinction be-tween fact and value. At the base of the understanding of this distinction is the perception that values in some way come from individuals and cannot exist in the world, at least not in the world of frogs, car batteries, and coins. If they did, then they would be like rocks, guitar strings, and orthodontic de-vices and would not be values at all. And so I raise the ques-tion of whether it is possible for a statement to be considered a fact since, in fact, it is issued by an individual. And compound this with our need to establish the statement as valid before we will consider it as possibly a fact, itself an evaluative move, and you can see my problem. Well, one of my problems, as my biggest problem is that I think like this—about the simplest things, but nothing is really simple, is it? The whole fact/value thing was my way of arguing that my wife's claim that giv-ing up drinking would be good for me was not a fact, but a value judgment. Then I added for effect and for something else, though I don't know what, that my desire to drink, as an unspoken thing in the world, as an animal sensation, was in fact, fact and not a statement of value, and since the sensation did not depend on an individual for its derivation, then my de-sire for drink was more real than her assertion that stopping would be beneficial.

She replied, "But your desire has now been articulated and so has become a value statement."

***

Sally: What was that noise?
Ishmael: I didn't hear a noise.
Sally: You must have heard that.

Ishmael: I heard nothing.

Sally: Well, I did.

Ishmael: What did it sound like?

Sally: I don't know.

Ishmael: Where did it come from?

Sally: From the basement, I think.

Ishmael: That's where a noise would live. If there were a noise, it would be there.

Sally: I'm sure I heard something.

Ishmael: I'm sure you're sure. I'm sure you heard something. You're not mad.

Sally: I wouldn't be so sure.

Ishmael: I'm sure. We can't both be mad. Why would you think you heard something if there was nothing to hear?

Sally: That's true. I suspect it was a normal house sound.

Ishmael: It must have been that.

***

"Nothing happens at random, oll happens out of reason or by necessity."

This is the one sentence of Leucippus's *The Great World Order* to survive and make it to us. You will note the typo in the fifth word, following the comma that should have been a semicolon. Is it in fact by reason or by necessity that I have made this mistake? Is it merely a device that allows this portion of the discussion, a term I use loosely, or is it, and here some reckoning with the fictive space between this treatise and me and between me and the author is required, a random event, in so much as a typo can be considered an event, that allows me to make use of it? However much this notion aligns Leucippus's thinking with Anaxagoras, it does not suggest the beginnings of atomism that Leucippus is credited with putting forward. "After the fact" is an important, necessary concept, if not even, as we have seen, micro and macro, in human history—a worldview.

***

Naming functions as a device for distancing as much as a emblem of connection. Name. Naming. Named.

***

The practice of waterboarding was once refered to as the water cure. The subject is bound (as in *tied up* not *headed for*) in my case with duct tape, the silver kind made by 3M, to a board, mine being a fir plank, truly flat and without a knot, with his head positioned lower in elevation than his feet, taped up tight so that he cannot move and then a rag, in my case a side of a burlap feed bag, light brown with some lettering (the sack contained corn mash that I fed to wild turkeys in winter), is tied tightly over his face, and then water is slowly poured onto the cloth. The subject, I prefer the term to *victim*, has trouble breathing and becomes fearful (a rather mild word in this circumstance, but it serves to underscore my detachment from the reality of my action) that he will drown, that he will die of asphyxiation. He tries to squirm, but he cannot move, his stomach muscles jump as if zapped with electricity, his head violently shakes and hardly moves in turns, his eyes tear, I take this on faith as I cannot see them, and he tells you things he thinks you want to hear, muffled though they may be through fabric and fear and water. Those who are good at the practice, an odd stand-in for *adept* in this instance, at administering the technique seldom lose a subject to death; the lungs being higher than the mouth, it would be hard to get water into the lungs, or so goes the reasoning. Waterboarding leaves no marks cuts scratches or bruises, leaves no trace no evidence, only the whimpering complaints of its subjects, and the sweet remembrance of the torture's author.

***

I am on my way to New Mexico from Los Angeles, driving my car, the one I pay taxes on, California tag 5BFJ741. There is a body in my trunk. Put out an Amber alert, boys, there's a body in a trunk. There is a live air-sucking saggy-shouldered woefully unslaked (in so many ways) hairy-knuckled droopy-scrotumed human body in the trunk of my car, which may or may not be worse than having a dead one in there. There is a man's breathing yet breathless body in my trunk, and more than just his trunk is in my trunk, but his arms and legs and head, his face and fingernails, his past present and future, and every dream that he has ever dreamed he had. All back there, stowed against the noise of the highway and my spare tire.

There is a body in my trunk and Thomas Jefferson's ghost is sitting beside me, in the passenger's seat, and he is smoking an absurdly large joint. He is taking long slow founding-father drags and breathing out declarational clouds and constitutional rings of smoke. His eyes are sex-with-a-slave-glazed and peaceful.

"I grew this weed," he says. "Gardening is the greatest thing we can do on this earth." He offers me a hit.

I take it, but I don't put it to my lips.

"Have some," he says. "But don't nigger-lip it."

I look at the joint between my fingers.

He says, "Beautiful evening. Beautiful sky."

"There is a man in the trunk," I tell him. I give him back the joint and watch as he relights it.

"What are you planning for him?"

"Haven't decided."

Jefferson nods. "I wrote once that force is the vital principle and immediate parent of despotism."

"That sounds very wise."

"I thought so. Tell me, did you force the man into the trunk of your car?"

"I did."

"I see."

"And despotism is bad, why?" I asked.

"I didn't say it was bad. I never said it was bad. But remember"—he tokes on his joint—"democracy means that 51 percent of the population can shit on the other 49." He coughs. "This is some good stuff."

"I believe somehow that you're here, but I don't understand why you're here?" I asked.

"Does that really matter? Perhaps, my dark friend, I'm here to serve as some kind of curious metaphor. What kind, who can say? Not that it matters, but I said that. Or maybe I'm here merely as a standard against which to judge the standing, barely standing, president. I was interested in philosophy and architecture, he in fart jokes and cocaine. I founded a university; he barely graduated from one. My little prop here of the marijuana cigarette, well, I've got to do something while I'm here. Perhaps I'm here only to say, heavy-handed device and all, that you people have really ruined whatever opportunity you had to make this country special. Not that things were ever really any better; greed, stupidity, vanity have long and robust histories. It's not that you really ever had a chance. And that's the real sadness; you one and all eat up the myth-eaten nonsense we spouted back when slaves were slaves and owners were owners and fail to acknowledge the hard, cruel realities of human frailty and selfishness. You're all so painfully dull and pedestrian."

I laugh, considering his last remark.

"All this forefather nonsense. Tell me, are you going to kill the man in the trunk? Really?"

"Probably"

"Tell me, my friend, what do you think *cruel and unusual punishment* is?"

"I suppose I'd have to know first what is not *cruel* and what is *usual*. If *not* cruel is *kind,* then is it in fact punishment? And it seems to me that *kind* punishment sounds a bit *unusual.*"

***

"Shan't," said the cook.

***

Language is like a disposable ladder, one that once we achieve our level of meaning we kick away and wonder how we got to where we are. Werewoof one kinnot speak, theiroff one mist be soylent. All this while we play and pain with a language that is private. A draught peered into the old winkinstein.

Rung after rung after rung after rung after rung after rung after rung after rung after rung

To meaning dogs

Grammars laid side by side, the bell rung ladder ring rung rigged to fall to fail to bail to boil to boll to roll to role to rove to love.

Swiftly now drink sternely from thy stein.

***

Sally shows up at the precise minute her letter said she would, in a rented convertible, a red Ford something, with six wasteful cylinders, and as she revs the engine up the last forty yards of steep incline I can hear that the engine is missing just a little, that maybe a lifter is shot. Her dyed blond hair, false color covering gray rather than dark, blows in with what little breeze the day offers, coming from the west, up the mountain, through the trees.

"Hello, Ishmael!" She is cheery, always cheery, but never quite happy, and she will be even less happy with me shortly. She is dragging her as-big-as-she-is Louis Vuitton bag out of the backseat of the topless car.

I take the bag, put it down, and hug the rail that is her body, feel her shoulder blades against my forearms, her clavicle digging into my chest. I ask about her flight.

"A flight is a flight is a flight. Except now the attendants are men and far prettier than the women ever were. They're prettier than I ever was, that's for sure. Whatever happened to the overmade-up little stewardesses of the seventies that pilots used to leave their wives for?" She surveys the front yard, the big tree on the side, the swing hanging from it.

"I don't fly," I say.

"You're a sad case, Kidder."

"So you tell me."

"So I tell you." As if to say it is her business to tell me, that she will tell me again and again because it is her business. "Are you still not eating in restaurants?" she asks.

"I'll eat in restaurants, but I won't eat their food. I prefer to take my own."

"I forget, is it because you're afraid of being poisoned? Who are you? Camille Claudette?" She is walking in front of me toward the front of the house. Her left heel is slightly loose, and so when she brings it around it looks to turn toe-in but lands toe-out, disturbing the soil as it does.

"As a matter of fact. Have you ever been in one if those restaurant kitchens? And where has the food been before that? Meat hacked up by underpaid people without benefits who could care less whether feces splashed on the flank steak or not. No, thank you, I'll eat what I kill and what I grow."

"What have you killed? You're no hunter." Sally stops at the gate and looks back at the sloping pasture. She lights a brown cigarette, then puts it out immediately, using her loose-heeled shoe to smear it into the ground.

"I know hunters." But I am looking at the litter she has dropped. I pick it up and put in my pocket.

"And you trust the meat they, these hunters you know bring you?" She opens the gate and moves to the door. On the stone walk I can see and hear that she drags that shoe.

"I trust them. I don't do the killing myself. There's no shame in that."

She looks at me, failing to see the hunter in front of her, failing to see her failure at seeing my failings, failing to smell the blood on my breath, failing to hear the lie that floats between us.

Inside the house she looks around. She tells me I'm a pretty good housekeeper for a man with such an untidy mind, so she resists pulling a finger across a surface to inspect for dust. She stops at the mantel and points a skinny unpainted nail to a large wad of tape. "What's this?"

"It is a large wad of tape," I say.

"I can see that."

"Then you know what it is."

"What's under the tape?"

"You tell me."

***

Man X is identical with Man Y. Man X = Man Y. If Man X has properties P, P1, P2 . . . Pn, then Man Y has properties P, P1, P2 . . . Pn. Still how is this contingent statement of identity possible? Is Man X Man Y, and if so why is there a Man Y at all? With my vengeance eyes burning the horizon for Man X, will Man Y do, and will he satisfy my desire, and am I correct not only in my identification of Man Y as Man X, but also in my belief that there is a Man X at all? In other words or at least in my words I am questioning the notion that a thing is necessarily self-identical. The question is: what kind of question is this? What kind of assertion is this? The things we think when we think to kill. Killing X = Killing Y?

But is this lowly Y a member of a set such that one of the attributes is that Y is not X? And is there a class of such members, Y, such that if Y is not identical to all members of that set which shares no attributes with X, then there might exist some Y that is in fact not a member of that set?

The man I torture is not me, but he is a member of that set of individuals that are capable of a crime of which I am incapable, but is he, by virtue of his unique guilt, not a member of that set with which he shares that all important attribute of sharing no attributes with me? When I kill him will I be diminishing the number of members of that set of individuals capable of killing a child such as my daughter or will I be extinguishing the only member of a set that has only one member and is defined as belonging to that set by its identity, namely the attribute that he is of the set alone?

Fuck it. Just kill the motherfucker.

***

***

It is the dissymmetry in the natural world that creates beauty, the fact that a thing cools down, but will never heat up without an input of energy, that a rock will stop rolling, but will not start without an input of energy, that the days lose meaning and will not mean anything new without an input of energy. If I was not paid for my writing, then I would not have food,

I would not have energy, I would cool down to ice and cease to move. And the days would mean nothing. That much is clear. Yet sometimes I hate the view so much. Itisthe dissymmetry ofnaturethatcre ates beauty the factthatathingcools down

***

The cleanly cool desert morning made the drive from Los Angeles back to New Mexico feel safe. Interstate 10 unfurled in front of me as I drove toward the sun. The big fish in my trunk hardly flopped at all. What ideas might be russelling in his white head?

The window was partway down and the cool air was reminding me to remain awake, reminding me to remain on the road, reminding me to observe the speed limit. I considered the notion of a limit to my speed, an imposed limit. My speed at what moment? My average speed? What if I drove ninety, then fifty, then eighty, then sixty? Wouldn't I have been observing the seventy-miles-per-hour speed so-called limit? But the trooper wouldn't care about my speed, vectors, velocity, only about the thumping sound coming from trunk.

"What is that noise?" he would ask.

"That would be the man in my trunk."

"What's he doing in there?"

"Hopefully, not much."

"Does he want to be in there?"

"I can't imagine he does."

"Hmmmm."

"Hmmmm."

"Would you mind stepping out of the car, please?"

"Okay."

"Would you open the trunk for me?"

"Certainly," I would say to him. I would reach down and pull the little lever between the seat and the door. Then the officer and I would walk around to the back of the car.

Where the cop would say, "Well, you were telling the truth. Mind telling me why you've got him in there?"

"He's the man who raped, tortured, and killed my eleven-year-old daughter."

"What do you plan to do with him?"

"You don't want to know," I would say.

The officer would then close the trunk and tip his hat to me. "Watch your speed, okay?"

"Thank you, officer."

Then as I was falling in behind the steering wheel, the policeman would step to the open door and ask, "Are you sure you have the right man?"

"No, I'm not."

"You have a good day, sir. God bless America."

***

Heraclitus did not think much of people. Sage. He possessed a rather low estimation of the human capacity to understand what he had to tell them, or what was right in front of them for that matter. So, perhaps his so-called fragmented style is one meant to cause puzzlement, a kind of jump start (please excuse the anachronistic simile) to thinking, a clipped input of energy. Some historians suggest this very thing, and they suggest this because they are dunderheads and, like Heraclitus's lowly held comrades, they simply don't get the point and so seek a rationalization for that failure. I like to imagine that he wrote the fragments to be just what they are, fragments, and not shards from a grand work, all of them of a piece because they are, after all, fragments, but as fragments, they are also, necessarily, not a whole.

Heraclitus did not think much of people. This is not the same as: Heraclitus did not think of people much. The former might be the result of the negation of the latter and then be, in fact, a truth that leads to the latter.

The cat tells me I may take this road or that one and that either will get me to a place to which I will be going. The March Hare is that way. The Hatter, the other. My direction matters little. They're both mad. And the cat? He fades back in.

***

Today, my friend, we play a new game. Yes, a new one, a brand-new game. You're going to have to learn to relax and enjoy these games, that's really all there is to it. Well, there is more to it than that, there of course always is, but none of that matters to you, at least it can't matter to you, not that it shouldn't, it probably should, but it can't. That's simple enough. Today I will be your therapist. I know, the old joke jumps right out at us, doesn't it? I'm going to be therapist to the rapist. Aren't words marvelous? Anyway, I'm your doctor, your head-shrinker. That's the game. And my name shall be Immer Weider, and your name shall be, let me see, yes, Negatio Omnis. I am the famous Austrian psychiatrist, and you are my poor suffering Italian peasant patient whose miserable and pitiable plight will make my illustrious career. Let's get started. I do believe all the mirrors are in place. Good. Of course our sessions, as you probably imagined, will be a little different from other similar activities, as I'll be doing all the talking and you will remain happily silent and yet somehow we will get to the bottom of your trouble, the depth of your meager being, the floor of your cluttered conscious mind, the substratum of your slovenly subconscious, the underbelly of your untidy unconscious. First of all, let me give you some bad news. I'm not a Freudian. So, any hope that you might have had of excusing your behavior because of a lack of motherly cuddling or a predominance of phallic symbols in the culture around you is pretty much out of the question. A building often must be higher than it is wide. A cigar, well, that might be a different story, but nonetheless. The space into which the building rises is never a problematic vaginal construction, however much you might find comfort in thinking that I might think that you think that. It matters a mound of blue nothings to me that you have absolutely no idea what I'm talking about.

Let's talk about your childhood. I'd say you were touched by an alcohol-stinking uncle when you were twelve or so, not really an uncle, he wasn't related to you by blood, but a cherished family friend you were encouraged to call uncle even though you were always slightly uncomfortable around him. So, he touched you. No, he came close to touching you, to touching your little uncircumcised prick, his big hairy fingers near your hooded and frightened willy, came close, and you had a bad dream about it and wet the bedsheets, and your father came in and beat you. Your father beat you with a braided leather belt while your little sisters, gowned and bare-footed, looked on, a little scared, snickering slightly, and the belt accidentally grazed your delicate little testicle, and you screamed out and cried like a baby, and your younger sister laughed out loud, and so you started hated little girls, and that is why you're where you are right now. But all of that tells me nothing, does it? Does it tell you anything?

Let's try the mirrors. Mirrors and metaphors, that's where our answers lie. Answers lie. Isn't language beautiful? What is between you and the mirror, the first mirror, if in fact you can actually see that one in particular, if you can in fact see a mirror at all and not merely your reflection? What is between you and your first reflection? Space? The glass of the mirror? That which makes the glass a mirror? You know, you never ever touch or even face the thing that stands in opposition to you, only that which is between you and that thing. You only have experience with the between. But if the between is the thing to which you attend, then what is between you and the between? And what is the between between the betweens? Zeno, Zeno, Zeno. The number of points between here and the moon is infinite. The number of points between you and the door is infinite. Infinity equals infinity, and so the door is as far away as the moon. Still, if we both started walking right now, together, at the same time, I'd make it to the moon before you made it to that door. But that's not so much beside the point as it is between the points and so, as you now know, there is always room between points. For most of us, it's not the between that's the problem, it's the points that are hard to find. Glance at your reflections however, and you'll see that you can't find the betweens, and yet you're hard pressed to touch the points. So, where are you, Negatio? Did you know him well? There you are again and again and again and in order for you to appear you have to dissociate yourself from everything around you, but you can't do that, can you? And if you can't appear, then you can't know that you are, and so where is your being? And, and, and what a terrible mess for you, Negatio. Alas.

I've been thinking, as I'm sure you have, and I know you wish I'd stop, about sensations, about how we can't really share them. All we share is the relations between one sensation and another and one's self. So, really the only objective truth (how I hate the slippery notion of objectivity) is in relations. That is the singular way we understand the world, Negatio, and therefore ourselves, by regard of, consideration of, appreciation of, measurement of mere relations. This is what I'm taking from you, stealing from you. The sad part is that as I take it from you, I might be taking it from myself, perhaps from everyone. That is a sad thought, isn't it? But it can't matter to you. I'm not saying it shouldn't, but it can't.

***

***

The words on these pages are not the story. The words on these pages are not this story. The words on these pages are the words on these pages, not more, not less, simply the words on these pages, one after another, one at the beginning and one at the end, bearing possibly some but probably no relation to each other, but they can, if you desire to find a connection, need to, or if it irresistibly, axiomatically, ineluctably reveals itself to you. When you leave, desert these words, the words on these pages, you might use words very much like these to report what meaning you have found, but not these very words. You perhaps will leave these pages, the words on these pages, with an idea or two and maybe, just maybe, the order of a few of these words and so it goes.

I am not interested in what meaning you will make when reading the words on these pages, if you chose or can make any meaning at all, but in the limits of what meaning you can make. Humpty Dumpty notwithstanding, the authorities of my homeland notwithstanding, you cannot make words, symbols, signs mean just anything you like. So, where are the constraints? By whose arbitrary rules do we read? Are they rules of inference, and why is it that we adhere to them, without knowing why we obey them, without being able to articulate them? The words on these pages are not a story. You may have them if you like.

***

ASTERISK ASTERISK ASTERISK

***

I met a man on the street and he asked me if I believed in god, and I told him I did not. I think my actual words were, Fuck you. He then asked me how it felt to have no faith. I smiled. I have faith, I told him. Every time I get into my car it is only faith that has me believe that the other idiots on the highway will not drive straight into me. It is faith that allows me to believe that when the doctor is giving me a tetanus shot that he is not injecting me with heroin. It is faith that allows me to believe that when I put my money in the bank I will see it again. Of course I refuse to eat in restaurants. Faith is faith. Stupidity is stupidity.

How long is a meter? Well, it's one hundred centimeters. How long is a centimeter? It is ten millimeters. And how long is one of those things? But for the sake of argument, let's stop there. Who gets to say how long a millimeter is? I have many rulers, and I apparently trust all of them. These things are manufactured by different companies. Why are all the millimeters the same? And why do we trust them to be the same? There is some standard housed in some room in some building in Paris and let's call that standard the Golden Meter or, better yet, the Golden Rule. I like to think of it as a spatial imperative. But there it is, glimmering in its glass case set upon a granite pedestal. The Acme Ruler Company of Chino Hills, California, did not send a representative to Paris to use the Golden Rule to make a template that they then took back to the factory so that Acme rulers would be true. In fact no ruler company ever advertises on its package that their product is accurate. They know we believe in them. The tape measure might not retract smoothly, but by damn an inch is an inch is an inch. No, the Acme team used a Zenith ruler bought down the street from the drugstore to make their template. How accurate are any of the things we use to measure? Even the smallest influence on the act of transferring the length of the meter from one place to another can alter it. *Can* alter it. Even the mere pressure of our observation, the insignificant weight of our gaze. So, how many times removed is my *trusty* Acme ruler from the standard? Is this the reason why no house is square? How can it be anyway if space is curved? I have faith that, for all practical purposes, my meter rule from the Acme Company will closely enough approximate a meter that I can build things that fit into this world with other things. That is where my faith lies, in the fact that for some reason some things will fit together and work. I have absolutely no faith that the units of measurement of this world are true.

* * *

I come back to the question, as I always come back to the question, how is it that I am I, or me, the I or me depending on whether the first I is really *I* and not merely some word "I" designating another "not *I*"? One thing I am not, as in the consideration of natural kinds, is a conjunctive list of attributes that when taken all together make me an instance of me and perhaps only me. Any number of men have my same birthday, were married on the same day, in the same city, had a child on the same day, perhaps even lost a child on the very same day, but, finally, not to the same predator, not in the shade of the same shrub, not sniffed by the same dog. So, there are two things that mark me as distinct, as the individual *thing* that I am: the death of my daughter and the particular location in space. The notion, the claim, even the reality of my daughter's death is a vapor, cannot be touched, and so the only real identity I have is my spatial orientation to the rest of the world.

* * *

"I don't know what kind of dog it was," the detective said, without the least bit of irony or even judgment of my question. "One of you will have to come down and see the body, to identify the body." Of course. It was so simple. One of us would have to do that. One of us.

I looked at Charlotte's retreating gaze. In that second I recalled the feeling of loving her, of making Lane, of loving Lane with her. And then I looked at Charlie, the boyfriend, and I saw him loving her not unlike the way I had, and I put my hand on his shoulder and told the detective that I would be going downtown to do the identifying.

That's what I did. I identified my daughter. For the first and last time in my life, I identified my daughter. I had spotted her many times, on playgrounds, across rooms, in crowds of children. Once when she was costumed up like an elf among other elves I had even recognized her, but I had never identified her. And as I stood there in the medical examiner's surprisingly warm room, I realized that I did not recognize her, that the thing I was identifying was no one I knew, and I wondered if there was something to all that talk about spirit and soul. Then I looked again, and there was my daughter, there was Lane, both identified and as recognizable as she had been three days earlier, except that she was now dead.

"Yes," I said to the detective, "that's my daughter. She's all there." I didn't know why I added that, except that somewhere in my mind I imagined the police still out there looking for some piece of her. I was no doubt saying it to myself so that I would in fact stop searching. But of course I wouldn't; I would scan the eyes of every child I would meet, seeking some bit of my little girl. I knew this as I walked from the identification and across the parking lot. I also knew that after one or two more times, I would not see Charlotte again. We would become painful reminders for each other, and also, our last remaining connection in the world was gone.

***

The much-talked-about and never-seen nothing machine does nothing. The white-coated, name-tagged, spectacled technician puts you into it, switches it on, and nothing happens and, especially, most notably, nothing happens to you. You step into the machine, and you step out. You ask before what will happen, and the technician adjusts his thick glasses and says, "Nothing." You ask what will happen while you are inside the machine, and the technician scratches and says, "Nothing." You ask if anything will happen if you don't go into the machine, and the technician says, "Nothing." You look at the machine, and it looks like something, a big something large enough for you to enter, but it does nothing, so you are told, and it is after all the nothing machine, and you ask what will you experience differently if you don't go into it and let the dutiful technician switch it on. "Nothing," he says. You ask what you will experience differently once you come out of the machine, and the white-coated, name-tagged technician removes his glasses and peers out the window at the mackerel sky and says, "Everything."

***

***

Take this as an apology of sorts as we sit here in this close, dank down-below, in this arid region, in this hollow, toneless country, in this soulless culture that all your daily discourse about virtue, about values, worth and worthiness, about other things of which I hear you examining yourselves and others, none of that amounts to very much as long as your own life goes unexamined. You, my poor tied-up and gagged friend, are that examination, that assessment, that reckoning. You are also, sadly, importantly, necessarily (and that is the significant designation, *necessarily*, and not just, what I will call the logical variety of necessity, but a cosmic kind), the existential proof of the sincerity of my so-called convictions, among other things. I believe it is true, and this might be one of the ills of our culture, that no judge among us really has the courage of his convictions. I raise this glass, a mug really, filled with a moderately priced and nearly objectionable but finally, obviously, drinkable Shiraz that you will never taste, you poor bound-up and sock-stuffed bastard, you wretched futureless insect, if only you had an exoskeleton, and I ask where are you going, where have you been, where are you now, and where am I? Where am I? I might yet separate you from your soul, a kind of purification maybe, a relief, certainly a purgation. I suppose it depends on the pattern or practice of your soul, your umbra, if you'll allow that. Wouldn't you say? If you could say. No matter. We're going to separate something from something. You can believe that.

✳✳✳

Charlotte and I had divorced years before, and our different expressions of sorrow and grief served to underscore why our decision to part had been a reasonable, if painful, one. After the astoundingly shocking and surprisingly tedious medical examiner's report depicting in such minute detail the abuse inflicted on our daughter and the suggested cause of her death, as if it was something other than "the monster found the child," Charlotte surrounded herself with family and friends, an understandable and predictable course and perhaps the correct one, but I chose to retreat from anything with a voice, certainly from anyone whose voice might speak to me with some familiarity. At Lane's funeral, Charlotte and I hardly exchanged glances, much less words, and somehow the nature of the glances was in some way accusatory, though I was not accusing and I believe neither was she. But I could feel it, and I knew she could feel it as well. I also knew that it was unfair, incorrect, a function of despair, this phantom accusation, but absolutely inevitable, and, so, uncomfortable-making and necessarily damaging, though at some point in the deterioration of a thing any consideration of damage becomes moot.

***

F u fiend thieves pages punny, knough that they mean so futile as to plead useless. I mean no harm, as in jury, no disrespect to any tow home I might allude, but such a dark tail flicks on few lights. So, see the leaves not as dark, but as a raid of light upon the pratticks of our people, yes, our people—tower steeple, from where we get the worts from the pulled pit, the righteous permission to skin the cat, to exact the measure, to hold no quarter. But find it kind of fumy, a blow to the belly laugh, a kick to the head.

***

President: Pull my finger.
Secretary of State: Hey, that's not your finger.
President: Eh, eh, I know. Nothing happens if you pull my finger.

***

I'm down here in this underworld looking for my meanings. Have you seen them? Are they under this table? No. Not here. Are they behind this rickety cabinet? I'm lost without them, my meanings, my meanings of vast reduction, my dear meanings that lately seem to do whatever they like anyway. Perhaps they are here behind this portmanteau. No. What is that dripping? Dripping in this cave. Linguistic condensation? They're in here someplace, somewhere, someway, somehow. Occam's waiting in a dark and dank corner with his sharpened razor, waiting to cut a few throats, cut, slit, slash, slithy, thwack.

* * *

Theaetetus: I do not undertake to argue that madmen and dreamers think that they are gods and that they can fly and that they are flying in their sleep.

Socrates: Do you see another question that can be raised about this, specifically about dreaming and waking?

Theaetetus: What the fuck are you talking about?

Socrates: A question that you've heard often. How do we know when we are awake and when we are asleep and dreaming?

Theatetus: Don't you know the difference?

Socrates: Of course, but how do we distinguish between the two?

Theaetetus: Don't you know?

Socrates: Wait, I'm asking the questions here.

Theaetetus: Are you? Or are you dreaming?

Socrates: You're turning this all around.

* * *

Lane was riding behind me in the car. Air bags and all that. She was back against the right-side seat, her belt fastened, her face turned to the window.

"Daddy, do you love Mommy?" she asked.

"Yes," I said. I gave her a glance in the mirror, but she was looking away.

"Then why don't you live with us?"

"Because I want to continue to love Mommy."

I could hear her mind turning. "What about me? Do you want to continue to love me?"

"I will always love you," I said.

"What's the difference?"

"Difference?"

"Between Mommy and me."

"You're my daughter. Mommy was my wife."

She caught my eyes in the mirror. "So, you can stop loving a wife."

"I suppose you can." I turned onto Charlotte's street. "It's not something you choose, whom you love." I felt clumsy. "I love your mother."

That sour falsehood hung in the air of the car's air until we stopped in the driveway. I killed the engine and stared at the simple roundness of the steering wheel. We opened our doors and let the lie out.

* * *

Oh, but we will and we do and we must and nobody and nobody and nobody and nobody can stop us.

The sun is rising over the trees, and I am standing in the meadow in front of my house. I consider a person other than myself who is exactly like myself to the point that any given characteristic I might attribute to myself can also be attributed to that other, so identical that any one trait I attribute to myself *must* be attributed to that other. Are we identical? Even if at this moment we are having this very same thought. It is not the case that I may say something of one that is not true of the other.

Except for one thing, and this is significant: I occupy a position in space, a particular, peculiar, unique station in the cosmos, and the other does not. If we occupy the same coordinates of spatial location, however we choose to describe such a thing, whatever calculus we create to spatially designate, then the essential stuff of the other must be materially different from my own since it's able to pass through matter and all that. So, that other that was so identical is non-identical. But of course Estelle Gilliam and I occupy the same space, but not a single statement concerning me can be applied to her. My real and unsettling question is: *Whose space has been invaded?*

***

So virtue is knowledge. It is the same thing to know what is good as it is to be good. And I believe with all my heart that I know what is good. Gnow wee may axe howl men whoo jugheads rightlee kin beehive incontintnethee. Thehat he shoed beslave so wend he has noledge, sum saihe tis impassible; for tit wood be strainge—sew thaught Sourboxes—if wind noledge was inamain sumpting alice kid muster it and deerag tit aboot lick a SLAVE.

* * *

There are no witnesses (and in fact there never are), only he and I stand before you. You are and must be the judge (what do you wear under your robes?), and you stand before us or rather we before you, and how do you decide who is in the wrong? You listen to our elaborately detailed and messy stories; you patiently listen while we narrate what happened, and based on some discernible quality or quantity of qualities you will decide that one of our offered narratives is somehow more compelling than the other and therefore more believable and therefore, finally, true. Associatively, then, the more compelling the story the more true it is. What are the qualities of the truthful, more compelling rendering? Is it in the chosen or unconscious gestures? Is it an appeal to a great many details? Or to fewer well-placed details? Is it the cast of my or his eyes? Is it the presence or absence of passion in the telling? Must there be an affection for the telling itself? And finally, is it true that if my telling of the events is more believable then what I say is true? Finally, again, the question "Don't you believe me?" is not the same as "Isn't this true?" Can you say, "Oh, I believe you, but I don't think what you're saying is true," or, "Okay, I know what you're saying is true, but I don't believe you for one second"?

And well you shouldn't believe me. Never believe a man who doesn't give a damn. Don't take water from a man who cares nothing of your thirst and don't have sex with a person who doesn't love you and don't laugh at a joke-telling imbecile who hates punch lines but loves setups.

Two terrified people walk into a church. One of them is a victim. The other is not.

***

Every child is an
   innocent
Each child iz an
   innocent
Each and every child
   is an innocent
Any child is an innocent
A child is an innocent
            all
Children are ∧ innocentz

Children are always
   innocents

Children are
   innocents

***

Excuse me while I shove three fingers to the second knuckle down my throat. The rejection of the referential object as an element in Saussure's semiology serves to articulate the dyadic character of the sign, *the linguistic sign unites, not a thing and a name, but a concept and a sound-image,* there is nothing but the signified and the signifier, everything functions entirely within a system of signs, such a semiological system is the only thing giving structure and therefore meaning to the world, so the object of reference is excluded from semiotic consideration— as Berkeley steps out of the way of the approaching carriage, as I sit quietly and address my dead child and what signifies my pain and guilt, guilt for feeling inadequately not enough pain and what unties me from the sign I have chosen from the sound-image that supplies a kind of background music to this movie with no moving the object to which I always refer, but which in this world has no referential designation, and there is a vermilion flycatcher not four feet from me, and she really shouldn't be here, there is no water here

***

The structure of my romance novels was confining, of course, but what else could I expect, knowing that my business was not art (that big and nasty word) in any way. But when would my business be art, and when would form and structure not confine me, not constrain me? So, even in my romance novels I had to find some kind of freedom and who is to say what the form cannot allow? Who is to say that in the middle of it all I cannot stop and say that the red of the male vermilion flycatcher is outlandish and gaudy while the mute color of the female gives us peace, or that my nation shames me as it rapes the world, as

Florida has its penis dropping down into the waters of if not innocent, then helpless people? Who is to say that here, right here, in my notes, book, whatever the fuck you want to call it, I cannot say that oil is the primary motivating concern of the stinking corrupt dumbass morally de-centered president and his greedy slimy ass-breathed henchmen? Who is to say that even though my claims feel and seem and sound naïve, even though I am preaching to the so-called choir (though none can sing and the opposition can't read), even though my fellow citizens are some of the dumbest motherfuckers to ever walk upright, that I cannot complain about the uncounted deaths of people who don't count (as in matter) or that I cannot burn the American flag? To ashes. All right here in the middle of what is a novel about something else. Is there really anything else? What, after all, when the day is done, when the fire's dying out, is a little rape among friends?

***

"'Give me your evidence,' said the king.
'Shan't!' said the cook.'"

***

I get water from up the mountain via a pipeline that leads into a two-mile-long, hand-dug ditch that traverses a gentle, winding slope through aspens and then through firs. It is a nice bit of engineering for which I can take no credit. Drug dealers specializing in marijuana and meth and who-knows-what-else, the real sort, these guys, not just pierced and tattooed wannabes, from down in the valley, periodically and dedicatedly come up to divert the flow of the creek from which I draw the water used to irrigate my pastures and water my gardens. There's a dam up there that stops the flow and fills a reservoir that feeds my pipeline that feeds my ditch that feeds my fields, and what the bastards do is return the creek to its intended and natural course, down into the valley where they grow their marijuana and run their labs.

The sweet and bewildered flycatcher believes the ditch is a waterway and so it is. The little bird lets out a stuttering *pit-pit-pit-pitty-zee!* No one answers.

* * *

So, Aristotle struggles with what Thales must have meant. I do not. Instead, I see full well the importance of *moist*. Of course there is moist and too moist, as during the Louisiana flood of 1927 or the tsunami of 2004. I am sure that more than one cheek-chewing redneck farmer said, spying his cow floating by on her way to the Gulf, "Things are a little moist for my liking." Water is the principle, the *arche* of all things and Earth floats upon it.

Of course the ascendancy of water had a bit of a history before Thales. Ocean and Tethys were said to be the parents, so to speak, of *becoming*, and there was that special water that filled the River Styx. But this is theological. Thank Thales for trying to remove the theo from the logical.

* * *

Therefore it is necessary to follow the common; but although the Logos is common, the many live as though they had a private understanding.

***

Somewhere behind the illusory transparency of words was my understanding of the novels that I made using the name of another person, a person I refuse to consider an alter ego. Also lurking behind these symbols, signs, marks is some clue to how my chosen medium might actually allow me to process or make peace with the world. Since the time of my child's death I had been unable to make any mark on any surface that might be my own, but somehow Estelle Gilliam found a voice and life, such as it was. Perhaps as a defense, I never felt a need to fully comprehend the language of my art, or rather what my so-called art might actually be, but in the absence of that voice, my voice, I could contemplate and study that language, attempt to map its loci, attempt to fix its place inside my being, my head, and, late at night, even make an effort to represent it with a crude kind of algebraic symbolism that finally, and not remarkably, always failed.

***

It was stifling hot at Guantanamo. It was always hot there. Marines marched around being marines. Cubans lived their lives on the other side of the impressive fence. Three crew-cut, muscled, narrow-eyed spooks-in-training rested after their cross-country run. One was from Canada, one was from Australia, and the last was an American. The Canadian opened the envelope that held their next training exercise. It said, simply: *Find a deer.*

The Aussie went off into the woods and came back empty handed. He said, "No deer out there, mate."

The Canadian went next and came back with nothing. He agreed that there were no deer in the woods.

The American went into the woods, was gone for a while, and returned with a rabbit.

"What's this all about?" asked the Aussie.

"That's not a deer," said the Canadian.

"Yes, it is," said the American. "Ask it."

***

"How do you know I'm mad?" said Alice.

"You must be," said the Cat, "or else you wouldn't have come here."

***

There are no screams in my world. Although my world knows no sense, because it knows no sense, because it is built upon articulate language, on the logic of syllogistic anticipation, on a calculus of familiar axes and patterns and remembered sequences and echoes. There are no screams. But I am not a timid poet. I control, compose, conduct, and constrain my words, perhaps not their meanings, but the words I manage, own them even, and I choose to employ them as sentries for my public and secret codes. Yet, and here is the rub, I am the thief, and I am already in the house. Here in topsy-turvydom a man can control his voice and words and yet make no sense and still have the senselessness of his utterances be true. He can stamp out and construct riddles round about and say that ideas smell like myrrh. He can coin a word and exact change and leave things as they were before. He can rhyme and scheme and skip and shout, but never can he scream. And he can make a poem while writing prose even though it seems obscene.

***

"Now, about this new book." Sally said. Late night. Coffee. Crickets. Moonlight. Windows. Creaking. Breathing. "Does it have a title?"

"Yes, it's called *The Gentle Storm*."

"Good, good. I like it. Damn, I love it. Is it done?" Crickets. Refrigerator's hum. Wind.

"No."

"Close to being completed?" Crickets. House boards settling. Breathing.

"No."

"What's it about?" Breathing. Whimpering. Wind. Crickets. Crickets.

"It's about what each and every one of them is about." I paused and studied her waiting face. "It's the story of Lucien Raines, a young painter making his ruthless way in New York society and of his sponsor Davida Hume and the love they deny and finally find only to have it cause so much pain for them and all those around them that they end it all in a suicide pact."

"Hmmm." Sip of wine. Crickets. "We might have to fiddle with the ending."

Breathing.

***

***

In the garden the lovely flycatcher perches, watching as I deadhead the roses, plucking wilted petals in fistfuls and letting them float like messages to the dirt. The little bird casually studies my hand as it folds into a ball then fan-fingers out into some kind of idea perhaps. All the airish signic of her dipandump helpabit, and I have finally accepted her seat there on that spindly branch, her assiduous presence. She stretches out her wings, letting the sun bathe them, so that I can see her breast, see that her chest is clean of graffiti, clear of symbols, free of meaning.

***

What motifs will sound to announce my arrival? Oboe? Horn? The popping of a snare?

***

. . . another protracted, ear-splitting tear, stick it to the wall behind me, and then I rip off another, and I watch his pale forehead wrinkle above the ragged edge of the tape, and as I examine the edge of it, a couple of threads fraying white from its silver, I think of my assertion that he is guilty and of his needless claim that he is innocent, and I consider the question of what makes any statement true, taking into account the factors of meaning and fact, taking into account lies and fictions, taking into account that no one gives a rat's ass anyway, but I entertain it all nonetheless, knowing that expecting my meaning to match the facts as a standard of truth rings of some kind of tiresome correspondence theory of truth, and of course that is just a shallow grave of a theory, the fact remaining that I am loudly tearing off strip after gut-stirring strip of my 3M duct tape like music in this deep damp room that is my basement, that is my world, that is my dark corner and cozy passage to light and sweet bedcovers and the freezing pit that is my stomach, my daughter's voice . . .

***

The Wind's Kiss
The Kiss of Midnight
Midnight Light
The Light of My Recovery
The Recovery of Passion
Passion's Return So Gentle

And soon in a grocery market, airport, train station, drug-store, beauty parlor near you:

The Gentle Storm

Of course, in my head, my least-cleaned room, in that world that remained mine, in that world of which these novels were but strange allegories, my titles were:

The Pressure of Observation
Deeper
Analytic of the Sublime
The Fundamental Concepts
The Principia
Other Languages Are All We Have

And soon, blah blah blah:

My Chosen Torture

But there is nothing in a title, nothing above and nothing below it, only pages behind it that don't remember it. The title is only ownership. That is why we apply them. I name you therefore you are mine. You are mine because I name you.

***

I might or might not have discussed Empedocles and Democritus. It doesn't matter. All things run mercilessly or mercifully together. Certainly, that's the point.

One (that would be me) can track the beginnings of philosophy as a concerted shift away from a rather naïve (primitive—a term I despise, yet choose to use it here because it might seem somewhat unexpected) anthropomorphic interpretation of the world and a logically predictable, if not necessary, diminishing concern with man as a moral agent. The divide is not clean and certainly not complete, despite my mini-alliterative blush. Heraclitus cared very much about the actions of people, as should we all. Even the Pythagoreans possessed a dual concern with the scientific explanation of the world and with the fulfillment of human moral possibilities. It is, therefore (how I love a well-placed therefore), not really true that man as subject begins with the Sophists, however there is a qualitative transition in Greek so-called thought. But is there a point? No.

Diogenes Laertius tells us that Protagoras of Abdera was the first thinker to point out that every experience has two logoi that stand in opposition to each other. That ain't bad. And coupled with Protagoras's belief that we cannot know whether gods do or do not exist, many factors playing into our inability to know, not the least of which being the shortness of human life, we are left with, me at its best perhaps, and my little daughter at its worst.

I occupy these sprawling solitary moments with a retracing, of sorts, of what they call Western philosophy so that I might make some sense of the world that I have been rudely thrust into and have had abusively thrust upon me. Food for thought is no substitute for the real thing, and so I sit here frantically motioning for traffic to pass me by while I contemplate *philosophy*. At the table with me, in this dream, if I may, are Walt Kelly, Samuel Beckett, and Sir Lawrence Olivier. They all want to know where dinner is, why it's so late. Beckett doesn't really believe that it's coming. Olivier is overacting as if he doesn't care. And Kelly, well, Kelly is making me laugh, telling me that he is a swamp silly dog, saying, "Birch! Birch! Birch!" because that is of course the only bark he knows.

***

I present, introduce, insert a rather tautological truth that one starts at the beginning, though at some pages into this one might wonder whether we are indeed at the beginning or approaching the end of one's rope or line, line being the operative pun (why be shy about it?). But of course given a Hobbesian metaphysical position (a move that is in itself arbitrary and, if not self-serving, then meant to cause a bit of consternation, but does offer up a point, that being that the rules are in fact mine to make up and that, if I wanted to, I could at the end of this paragraph enter into my initial discussion of, say, Freud without so much as a wink or a blink), our tautological truth is contingent anyway, our making use of our terms by our chosen rules, rather arbitrarily.

***

And what are my component parts (allow my redundancy)? If I were my chessboard, would one of my squares, black or white, be a component or constituent part of my whole, the board? If you found in my garden a single black square, would you wonder where the other thirty-one black squares and the other thirty-two white had gone? Is the edge of the board a part of the board? Is the paint? The inlay? And what about the shadows that fall upon the board in the evening? What about the history of games that have been played upon it? The game being played and the games that will be played? What about the metaphor I have made of it here? Upon finding the lone black square, some forensic scientist might examine the wood and discover that it came from the same tree as the other sixty-three squares of equal size, thirty-one black and thirty-two white, and so then is the chessboard a component part of that tree, and has it been a chessboard all along, even when in the tree? Could the wood that became my chessboard have become a tabletop instead? And likewise if you find me with that one piece gone, can you replace it and still call me the chessboard I was? Six pieces gone. Thirty-seven? And what if the pieces are all there, all present and accounted for, but disassembled? Let's play chess, I say and pull out my sixty-four squares, thirty-two white, thirty-two black, and drop them on the table. You ask, what is that? And I say, that is my chessboard. It's all there?

Lane: I found a beetle.
Charlotte: Let's see. Oh, he's a big one. What are you going
     to do with him?
Lane: I don't know.
Charlotte: Are you going to let him go?

Lane: I want him to mean something.

Charlotte: What? I don't understand.

Lane: I want him to mean something.

Charlotte: You want it to mean something to you when you let him go. Is that it?

Lane: I'm going to put him in a box. Let him sit for a while. Maybe he'll mean something later.

And so Lane put the beetle in a little box meant for earrings and used tape to secure its closure. She wrapped more tape around it. And more. She used all the tape and left the box hidden under the ball of plastic. She set it on the counter, then asked that it be placed on the mantel.

Lane: And we cannot take off the tape and open this box again. As long as we live.

And without telling us what the beetle meant to her, we were left with the knowledge, clear as anything in the world, that the beetle did mean something, and something different to each of us.

All there. All the notes. Thirteen in the scale. Eighty-eight on the keyboard. All the notes in the correct places, clinging to or lodged between the lines of the staff, melodies more easily recognized than not, chords properly placed, notes standing on each other. I cannot budge the notes, and so I am left with register and tone. Where do I put all of it, and how shall I have it mean?

***

＊＊

The joke is from skydivers. Who's crazy enough to jump out of a perfectly good airplane? Of course their answer is clear and easy enough, for the thrill, to overcome fear, that sort of thing. But suppose we're not skydiving, that we're flying from Denver to Santa Fe in a Beechcraft. What can you say to me that will make me jump out of this perfectly good airplane? That's where I was as I contemplated how my wife and I would divide the property and our lives, the two houses, the paintings, the library, and all those things, things, things. Things shoved out the open door of a perfectly good airplane, and I along with them, attempting to explain while trying to strap on my chute in midair why I am jumping, considering the bewildered looks of friends and family, what family there is, my daughter, and hoping, hoping through the tangle of strap after strap that I will get outfitted and land without too much of a thud on the ground near my reason for jumping. That's why one abandons the good plane, to find the ground, because you're tired of flying, because where you've been is fine and where you're going is fine, great even, but it's all in the plane, flying from Denver to Santa Fe, but headed north, the really long way to Santa Fe, with plenty of fuel, but still it's not on the ground and not near my reason for jumping. And how will I tell the other person on that plane that it's not her, that she is still wonderful, more beautiful than ever, but that she is not on the ground where I want to be? I will step from the plane and hope to experience that famed thrill of unaided flight, but I will simply be falling, at a steady and known rate, but falling, plummeting past high-flying geese, past particles of dust-encrusted ice, seeds for meteorological events, past anniversaries and birthdays, not one having gone unnoted, past the presentations of degrees and awards, the miscarriage, the birth, the death, past millions of "I love you's" and as many "You're the only one for me's," past erased insecurities, the shared friends, dreams, and nights of silly giggling. And somehow I imagine that I can endure the look on her face as I glance back at the rapidly disappearing plane, a perfectly good plane, imagine that I can expect her to understand. I will know this as I near the ground accelerating at the prescribed thirty-two feet per second. And once strapped on will my chute open, will I be high enough to land without shattering every bone in my body, will I land in the circle I have painted for myself on the planet? The ground, they will say, he never heard it coming.

***

Lucien wrote the letter three times, six pages of close-pressed cursive, beautiful on the page, and in it he found boldness more easily attained on paper than in speech. He wrote of his confused desires and of the terrible poverty of his youth. He sketched a picture of his sister as the angel she never was, and she had raised him in the absence of his mother by working two jobs, one of them seeming irregular in that she would never speak of it. It was one of those frantic letters in which young people threaten to kill themselves if their demands are not met, full of puerile casuistry and the unfeeling logic of conceited minds.

"This Lucien doesn't seem very sympathetic to me."
"Trust me."

***

***

"Reggie Reggie bo-feggie banana fanna fo feggie. I could never get that right. How are you this morning? Or night? You'll never know. Reggie, Reggie, Reggie. Let me set my coffee down here. So, how's it hanging? I just came down for a little chat. Rather, I needed an audience. You're game, right? Oh, I made a punny. I was upstairs making up limericks. Limericks, of all things. I decided to come down and share a few with you. A sip of coffee to wet the old whistle. Or is it whet the whistle? I can never keep that straight. Not that it matters a hill of corpses, I mean they sound the same, don't they? Okay, here's the first one:

> *There once was a man name of Reggie*
> *Who lived a life wild and quite edgy.*
> *He poked the wrong youngun'*
> *And now there is no one*
> *To save him from becoming a veggie.*

"Not bad, eh? Well, it was good for me. I wish I were more like you. Perhaps I could masturbate to all of this, you know, get off. Another sip of coffee and here's another:

> *There once was a man lost near Taos*
> *Who lived well deep beneath a house.*
> *It was fitting that he*
> *Should be bound so tightly*
> *To a board that he hugged like a louse.*

"Oops, place reference in the first line. Doesn't matter though. It's not like you'll ever be talking to anyone else. For the rest of your life. These last two I'm not so taken with. I hesitate even to read them to you, but what the hell. Where have you to go? They seem, seem, seem, I don't know, cold, wooden. But, you tell me. You're the critic here. Sip, sip.

> *There once was a father aggrieving*
> *Whose child got no love before leaving.*

No god came to help
With the pain that he felt,
So he wound up at home disbelieving.

"See, I told you about that one. A little, well, you know. And here's the last one, and then I'll leave you alone for a bit.

There once was a man with a daughter
Who returned home to learn of her slaughter.
He found her assailant,
Became his acquaintant,
And slowly did drown him in water.

"See you in a while, Reggie."

***

What is this Logos, this common, central understanding, this one, so reminiscent of Thales and Anaximenes and even Anaximander and his boundless. It is not water. Not air. It is, finally, fire. As always, when confronted with something that makes absolutely no sense being issued by a figure whose stature one wishes to preserve, the impulse is to claim impenetrability due to curiously curious paradoxes. Regarding some, I would offer that the paradoxes are at least the unfortunate products of a defective memory. Heraclitus wrote, fragmentedly, that knowledge of many things does not make men wise, but then he also held that men who love wisdom should "acquaint themselves with many particulars." Despite the fact that these two notions are not mutually exclusive, this notion is used by some to illustrate a paradox. But another beastly subtextual mission raises its head: often the meaning is so simple that one wishes to make it complex, as if complexity is a necessary trait of truth, or at least of significant meaning. Heraclitus *is* surface. This is my pronouncement. Paraphrase 1) Without a directed mission for knowledge, knowledge is useless. Paraphrase 2) A simple multiplicity of facts without a unifying understanding or design is pointless. Paraphrase 3) In the desert, the person who knows where the water is is a genius.

Water brings us back to fire.

All things are exchange for fire and fire for all things.

But fire reigns with a kind of burning symmetry. There is an equilibrium of the coming and going of fire. All things are in balance, proportionate. Fire is important, not because of its basic elemental status, but because it demonstrates to us the nature of opposing forces, the importance of the existence made possible by the tension between opposing forces.

Disease makes health pleasant; hunger satiety, weariness rest.

The path up and the path down is one path.

You cannot step into the same river twice.

The problem with understanding Heraclitus is that he has been misfiled. He was not a philosopher, but a poet. But you cannot step into the same pageant twice.

Not true, not true. Nature is so good at concealing herself (though she [I use *she*] never thinks to do so, perhaps cannot even think to do so) that you never know when or what the so-called *same* river or pageant is. Why, the same pageant could be right in front of you, if only you knew what the same thing looked like. Just as an object moving away grows proportionally smaller in our perception, seems to shrink in the direction of its motion, so the *same* must similarly be affected by the direction of its motion. Can two things move toward being identical? A little shaved off here, a bit of something added there. Are they nearing the same? Nearly the same? The same to begin with? Nasty, this sameness, and yet we return to it again and again and the same again. The same thing every time, or is it? Said same.

> *And tallweighs ooze sew large a feign*
> *That they kinknot be scene.*

***

What the fuck is redemptive value? And whose fucking value is it? What fucking gods am I attempting to appease and why? Who is fit to punish me? Why must I learn something? Why must I undergo a moral revelation? Why is it better to be good? Why must I question my actions? Why must I defend my intentions? Why must I weigh my effects? Why, again, must I be good? What's wrong with simply being even? Condemned to everlasting redemption? Will redemption be my penance? Will it finally be my crime? The moral high ground is not subject to flooding, but still it shakes.

***

I sit on the big, I believe, volcanic rock, and I am regarding my garden. My zinnias suck, I think. Would that I could grow nice zinnias. I love them not so much because they are large, but because they germinate so quickly. Mine never look the way I want them to look, but they are alive and so I love them, must love them. I imagine that I love them at least. I sit on the big rock and watch the flycatcher. The muted color of it is sweet in the afternoon light, the female usually less bright in birds, but there is something about this one. Perhaps because I am back-lit by the sun, she doesn't perceive me as a threat or perhaps doesn't perceive me at all. Then I consider human beings, and I realize that in fact I am a threat, a menace, perhaps only that in the world, and that this little bird should be afraid of me, she should know better than to perch too close. I step quickly toward her and she flies away. I feel as if I have done my part in this game, having imparted a lesson valuable and worthy of receipt. The hummingbirds come, but they belong here, too fast for anything, especially a clumsy fool like me, to harm them. They dart around, hover in front of me. The male shoots straight up into the sky, a whistling bullet of feathers and sex drive, while the female hovers and waits, unimpressed.

***

Slash slash whack whack cut cut. It's never as difficult as you think it will be. It never takes very long. It takes seconds. It takes centuries. It takes seconds.

> I'll kill thee everything I kin:
> > There is little to relate.
> I spotted and slashed a standing man
> > A-sitting on a gate.
> "Why are you standing, man?" I said.
> > "And how is it you live?"

And his answer bled through the room,
  Like water through a sieve.

***

***

I am not so distant from my concern with the truth as it appears or from my nagging concern with name relations, a concern that ironically has gone unnamed. I'd like to briefly take up the functions of negation, alteration, and logical conjunction. Are there any semantic criteria for such functions, any criteria for determining whether, say, a certain idiom is to be understood to express such a function? Negation is easy, as it merely turns something that agrees with the world into something that does not. Alteration is very similar to negation. But logical conjunction does more than merely compound things. It can create the possibility of contingency, of necessity, and of simple compounding, just as it compounds the problem. I am tempted to suggest, and you might say more than tempted as I am in fact, right now, this very second, suggesting that conjunction is the root of all human misapprehension and misunderstanding. To say that I am a father entails a necessary conjunction with a child, but given the negation of that child, am I to understand a negation of my fatherhood? Am I to imagine an alteration of the conjunctive relationship and a reconfiguring, therefore, of my relationship to the world. Without an *and*, am I in this place, at this time, in this body? Am I at all?

***

Gregory: You say you do not believe in witches and the devil?
Reasonable Person Like You: No, I don't.
Gregory: Why, that is tantamount to saying that you yourself are a witch.
Reasonable Person Like You: No, I don't believe it is.
Gregory: Certainly it is. What you're saying is that you don't believe in evil.

Reasonable Person Like You: No, I'm saying I do not believe
 in the devil as a being.
Gregory: Really. So, you don't believe that the devil is evil.
Reasonable Person Like Yourself: That's not what I said.
Gregory: You don't believe there is a devil and you do, you
 say, believe there is evil, so you are certainly saying that
 the devil is not responsible for evil.
Reasonable and Nervous Person: Listen, you're twisting my
 words all around.
Gregory: I think the rectal pear first for this one. Then the
 garroting chair. And finally a couple of days on the
 rack. We'll see if you believe in the devil this time
 next week.

Pope goes the weasel!

* * *

A signifier walks into a downtown bar carrying, but not di-
rectly touching a signified. The bartender says, "Hey, we don't
serve his kind in here."

The signifier says, "It's a signified."

The bartender says, "I was talking to the signified."

* * *

It was cloudless and sunny the day Charlotte and I brought
Lane home. She was small, they said, five pounds, but not that
small, they said, but I had never seen anything so small. I took
it on faith that those little fingers were complete with nails
and the very suggestion that they be trimmed with something

sharp sent me into a panic. A nurse had seen me studying them, one nail at a time, especially the little toes, and she, being one of those people who find comfort in nervous chatter, said, "Just wait until you have to cut them."

"Excuse me?" I said.

"You'll have to," she said. "Her little hands will be all over the place. If you don't trim her nails she might scratch herself. We wouldn't want that, would we now?"

"No," I said. I felt like I might cry.

Once in the house Lane began to cry. Charlotte tried feeding her, but she refused. She was wet, but a change didn't stop the crying. I kept looking at her fingernails and wondering if they were the problem. Charlotte called the doctor. An eternity later the doctor called back and told us that babies cry, but he offered to take a look at her. That was how he put it, "Bring her in, and I'll take a look at her," as if she were a car.

We took her to his garage, and he put her on the rack and listened and cooed and touched; he did have a way with babies, and so the baby stopped crying, and he assured us that nothing was wrong, and Charlotte asked, "Why was she crying?"

"Babies cry," he said.

"Why did she stop?" I asked.

"She got tired of crying," he said.

Back at the house Lane remained silent, had her feeding, and fell asleep. Charlotte and I stood over her, and the world had never been nor would again be so right.

* * *

Secretary of State: Pull my finger.
President: Okay.

I can do what I like at any moment I like in this document or text or however we name it because this is my world, universe, neighborhood, note (though I hate seeing the word note in my notes), and I can do what I damn well please and fuck you if you think I'm ignoring rules and fuck you if you think that I'm being indulgent and fuck you if you think that references to archaic philosophical notions are mere erudition, which they are not, but fuck you anyway because this is my world and you're welcome to it if you want to enter and if you don't want to enter then fuck you twice anyway and if you do want inside then fuck you trice because you fucking deserve it.

And thus did my hours pass in an unceasing vacillation between anger and absolution, between anxiety and appeasement, between validation and regret, preparations and despair, Ozzie and Harriet, Simon and Schuster, Leopold and Loeb, Abbott and Costello, America and Democracy.

My life without my daughter, without the presence for my reason for being, was merely, simply, only a *comédie à tiroir*. You goethe ta one drearer, opine it, thin toft to a nether, opine it, thin a nether, a nether, a nether.

***

Seven and sixty are now the years that have been tossing my cares up and down the land of Greece. And there were twenty and five years more my birth up, if I know how to speak truly of things. Such was the perhaps sad life of Xenophanes, expelled from his native Colophon and wandering hilly Greece and still wearing out the hide soles of his sandals in his late nineties. He was a satirist, his poems taking on Homer and the earlier poets, taking them to task for their depiction of the gods as sadly being like the humans who worshipped them. It bothered poor Xenophanes that the gods could get away with the crimes for which pathetic and frail mortals would be punished. He hated the cloying notion that gods might have had sex or that they might have worn clothes (on this point I can muster some sympathy). He pointed out that the Ethiopians worshipped snub-nosed, black, and dark-eyed gods, and that the Thracians put red hair on their gods' blue-eyed heads. He thought that if bears could pick up brushes and paint on the walls of their dens, pictures of their gods would be pear-shaped, clawed, and possessed of itchy backs and a pronounced taste for honey. The thrust of it all, the pointed philosophical upshot, was that Xenophanes offered the abandonment of anthropomorphism when talking about gods. He said that there was but one god, greatest of gods (a curious appositive, a little like saying, "this is the only apple in the bag and it's bigger than all the others") and men, a god that was in no way similar to mortals in bodily practice or in thought. This singular, greater-than-all-other-gods god never moves, but remains steadfastly fixed, for it would be woefully unfitting for him to visit or revisit different places at different times (but how about different places at the same time), but without much effort he can thunder-rattle all lesser things by the mere "thought of his mind." A fantastic king immobile on his throne. A fat, inert, lazy, unmoving, neglectful, constipated, slack-artist slob of a deity, toiling not, listening not, but causing all sorts of tribulation, tumult, and imbroglio by, well, merely thinking.

***

She yielded to him, though she didn't want to. His eyes were like fire, and she felt what little resistance she had left melting like snow on the hood of a minivan after a drive to the soccer field. He pulled her to his iron chest and breathed his delicious breath over her face. She couldn't help herself. She reached up and grabbed his hair, pulled her face up to his, and opened her mouth for his inquisitive tongue. He ripped off her blouse, buttons be damned as they skittered across the kitchen floor, and caressed her left breast, brushing her nipple with his callused thumb. He smelled of wood and gun oil and transmission fluid. She sucked in the air around him as his mouth found her neck. Soon they were both naked, and she on the counter. She looked down at the massive manhood searching for a den, and she supplied it, taking him slowly while she let out a wail that she hoped the neighbors couldn't hear. But damn them, just like the buttons, damn them all, let them hear!

A silver bullet (want to be sure it does the job) to my brain is what I consider as I read over this shit. If only I could keep my secret from myself. But then I'd probably be able to guess my own secret, wouldn't one think?

Sally is buried deep in sleep in the guest room, and I am sitting in my stuffed chair (it may or may not yet be stained with blood), as I do every night. I don't sleep, as always I do not sleep. I sit up awake and feel the weight of an imaginary pistol in my hand, the imaginary barrel in my mouth, the imaginary smell of gun oil in my nose, the imaginary edge of the trigger under my finger, the imaginary silver beast-killing bullet in the chamber. If only I were imaginary.

Cogito, ergo doleo.

***

I learned this, and I am not sure where and/or how but I learned it, and I believe (a notion far greater than knowing) it, that the present is extremely difficult to trace because it always moves at full speed. The past I can slow down, retard and recount, alter, must alter, necessarily alter, and the future I can stretch out into an extended waiting game, anxious or not, a restful procrastination, but the present is full tilt all the time, like the jittery electron and its sub-buddies, somewhere certainly, but where?

"Do you have a name?"

"Yes."

"Don't tell me. Names are always just substitutes for nouns, and you know what good nouns are. I will name you. I'll do that for you. The performative act of naming will be yet another little thing I do to you. I name you W. Poor, poor W. 'Where is W?' they are asking. 'Who cares?' others are saying."

"Why?"

"W, I am necessary. I am a necessary thing. My actions are all necessary here. Call it fate. Call it your god's word. Say it is in the stars. Say it is written. Think of it however you like. Think god knows it, if that helps you make sense of it. But I'd rather have you consider that I have renamed you Art and now you are Art and no longer W. My god, what have I done to you? Poor, poor W. now has a new name. Just like that, a new name."

It is here in this story that I am supposed to pause and offer some kind of humanizing history for this creature, something about his wretched childhood and obscenely behaving parents, molesting uncles and priests, and bouts with alcohol and drugs, whether true or not. He gets no story. This, if I have perpetrated any evil at all, is my greatest evil, my greatest vengeance.

"How about that, W.? I mean Art, I mean Harvey, I mean Mort, I mean—Isn't it wonderful? The naming of things? You get no story at all. But let me ask you this: Do you have a name?"

* * *

Man: Do you believe in God?
Me: I don't know what you mean.
Man: Do you believe there is a God?
Me: I have no idea what you're talking about.
Man: God. Do you believe there is one?
Me: What is this God you keep talking about?
Man: The creator of all things.
Me: What are all things?
Man: The world. Everything!
Me: I don't understand.
Man: Every single thing.
Me: Can you list them so I'll know what you're talking about?
Man: List what?
Me: Everything.
Man: You don't believe in God, do you?
Me: I don't know. I don't know what you mean by *God*. Let me ask you this, do *you* believe in God's father?
Man: That makes no sense.
Me: You know what God is, right?

Man: Yes.

Me: You know what a father is.

Man: Yes.

Me: How does *God's father* make no sense?

Man: Because God is the origin of all things.

Me: What about his father?

Man: His father has nothing to do with it.

Me: Whose father?

Man: God's father.

Me: I thought you said God has no father. Just whom are you talking about?

Man: You're upsetting me.

Me: You kant (and I say that with a *K*) stand it, can you, the fact that existence is not a predicate?

Man: I don't understand.

Me: Really?

***

Here I am, again.

***

Jerkgin Habermas rejlected Fraud or soak the storky glows. Perchaps on a coolefin oddning when the restled plages of chaste studies in a particularly annoidal way or evelyn rowmanic wale. Treble in his omasum? Behut are tall sexions parerga? At any rake, his saduction by Piggyjay and Kohldberg retempting to deconfinger Fraudian theirway to despict and remarkate a deafnight, if knot expressieve, scents of hisstory

and hystorical prattkiss incongrewus wit henyting omniver-
salistick and trainsindental in the cystame of Habermas.

***

*Man is the measure of all things, of things that are, that they are,
and of the things that are not, that they are not.*

Plato cites the above as the opening of Protagoras's *On Truth*.
Does it mean that what seems to be is and what seems to not
be is not? Does it suggest that we can know nothing? Does it
mean that without a subject there is no sense in the notion of
knowledge and therefore the world at all? Does this idea of
subjectivity apply only to perceived objects? Is it finally an appeal to the relativity of perception, a bow to a range of value
judgments regarding the perceived world? Is it an admission
to the solipsistic nature of existence? And what about moral
judgments? Is the *man* the individual or all of humankind?
For Plato, the sense of it becomes that things *are* true when
they are perceived, and that the perceptions of individuals are
equally true.

 This is a problem of course to a certain kind of rigid
mind. The fact that conflicting statements could be equally
true doesn't square with the principle of contradiction. In the
Metaphysics Aristotle writes, "We observe, next, that if all con-
tradictories were true at the same time of the same thing, it
is clear that all things would be one. For if anything may be
affirmed or denied of everything, then the same thing would
be a trieme, a walk, a man. For, if someone should hold that
a man is not a trieme, clearly he is not a trieme; then, if the
contradictory be also true, he is also a trieme." Whatever the

fuck a trieme is, things cannot be both true and false at the same time, I guess. But doesn't this argument employ the very notion of negation that it attacks? And why is it so important that knowledge be "fixed"? Well, it was certainly an assault of sorts on the earlier philosophers. And very difficult to swallow if your self-worth, station, power, position, and whatever else your investment in the world, is based on your knowing something that someone else does not know and might want to know, if you happen to be willing to share. More importantly, and this is what the Protagoreans of the world face, the Aristotles simply just don't get it. They get so busy with what X means that they forget to wonder why X should mean anything at all, or why we call X "X" or why we wonder why we wonder. It's no wonder that Plato presents Protagoras's story, his justification of, if not his existence completely, his function as a teacher, in the *Protagoras*, without a note of irony (he being deaf to such music).

Let me call this the Protagorean Theorem:

$$\text{knowledge}^2 + \text{certainty}^2 = \text{squat}^2$$

$$***$$

There was no good explanation. I should say that there was no good explanation that was true. I at times even tried to create a story, my artistic capacities sadly failing me, and perhaps that should have depressed me (but it didn't, as I had other dispiriting and dreary fish to fry), that might satisfy Charlotte's reasonable need to understand just what the fuck had happened to me. I imagined myself telling her that there was another woman, and I went so far as to try to find another woman, but finally it wasn't another woman, only me and my pathetic depression about maybe work, perhaps my life, but more just feeling day in and day out like I didn't want to continue. I no longer entertained suicidal thoughts, and that was ironically depressing as I could have used one right about then. Charlotte would look at me, as angry as she could be, rightly, and demand to know where I had gone, and I would look stupidly back at her, a sincere and true stupidity, however aggravating for her, and say, "I don't know." I became sick of saying I don't know. I hated hearing the words from my side of this face, but that was all I had. "Why aren't you happy?" I don't know. "Is it us?" I don't know. "Do you want to leave?" I don't know. Finally, without knowing anything, only that I was remarkably unhappy, I did leave, so clumsily and so awkwardly, at once thinking that a better person would have done it, well, better and that of course there was no "better," or even good way to break a kind person's heart. But everyday I was breaking her heart by merely being sad, by being absent, and no amount of faking could hide it, and it was affecting her and it was affecting my daughter and I had us all treading to keep our heads up in a stagnant stew and I hated every minute of it and I hated myself as well. I left saying the most unsatisfying and stupid and cruel and sadly true thing, which was "I still love you." It's funny how such *well-meaning*, selfish utterances often feel so benevolent. At any rate, my words were taken badly, an understatement, and I'm still unsure whether it was the "still" or the "love" that was so upsetting.

***

***

If I could have I would have, and it was done because I did. Whether I should have, it was not clear. That I ought not have was apparent as its being done was and is untrue to my nature, as I know it, and you can believe that if you can and will. Whether true blue or read back to front, the short long of it was easy to see since it was not there in the first place. Steadily, lip-partingly, rainbow-colored pig pass for a party at the president's mansion, not to mention declension and intention and some nonsense about sugar and spice and everything nice. And how it is that humans will never abandon religion? It is because the meaning is in the grammar of it all, because the grammar seduces, the grammar lies, the grammar makes you think that sense is there, the grammar sleeps with Grampa and Grampa is the cat's bowwow, the slithy sounds of a walrus, an earwig, a Hardly Comfortable Earwig. Late in the backseat of camel night a ywlbqx is turned and breath is made flux and you are made audv. Ysuwu dwu pn ywlbqx lp vlbylnp. Final impson flingalnix pumpdinkle foist malrump of tricks. Cdh jeheun o najsb ajhns iii ooo eee djnkfll.

***

There was a modest, rather inconspicuous shop on the corner. It was the only shop at the intersection. It was the only occupied corner. The other corners were vacant lots, one full of weeds, one full of piles of cardboard, and in the last one an old man sat on a stump. The old man wore a dusty red jacket and paid no particular attention to anyone and has no particular significance to this story. On the little shop was a sign that read:

WORDS

The young girl, the subject of this story, looked at the sign and wondered to herself whether she was reading the word WORDS or merely recognizing it. She imagined that there must be a distinction to be made between the two, but what? She walked inside, and the bell on the door announced her. She walked to the counter and addressed the tall woman standing behind it.

"Is this a bookstore?" the little girl asked.

"It is not." The woman put her hands to her head as if to adjust her hairdo.

The little girl looked around, and in fact she saw no books. In double fact she saw nothing but walls, a door set into the back one and windows into the front and empty shelves behind the counter.

"This is a wordshop," the woman said. "Do you have any money with you?"

"I have a dollar."

"That's enough for a few words, anyway. Depends on what ones you're interested in. Some are rather expensive. I don't have any that are free."

The little girl was intrigued. She wanted to know what the words would look like, whether they would come in a paper sack or wrapped in a box. "What should I buy?" she asked.

"That of course depends on what you'd like to say," the woman said, standing even taller.

"But if I could tell you what I wanted to say, then I'd already have the words I need."

"Be that as it may. Still, you can never have too many words. Make up your mind, little girl."

"Excuse me, but do you have a list or a catalog of some kind?" the little girl asked.

"Of course. What kind of shop would this be if I didn't have a catalog." The woman bent down behind the counter and came back with a big red book. On the cover read: DICTIONARY. "There. That's most of them anyway."

Then the little girl noticed a pile of small boxes on the counter, stacked neatly as a pyramid. "What are those?"

"We call those grab-boxes. There are four words in each one.

There is some repetition, but only some. But the fun is you never know what you're going to get."

"How much are they?"

"Fifty cents a box."

"I'll take one," the little girl said. She gave the woman her dollar and received her change of fifty cents. The woman handed her the box, and it felt so terribly weightless. "It's so light," she said.

"Words are like feathers," the woman said. "Only cleaner." She sighed as she peered out the front window.

The little girl took her new box of words out the door and into the sunshine. She couldn't wait to get home, so she tore into it immediately and found—nothing. She looked all around, feeling lost and somehow hollow, she thought. She was terribly and mightily and profoundly disappointed. She marched back into the wordshop and said, "THIS BOX IS EMPTY!"

"Those are fine four words," the woman said, smiling quite broadly. "You got quite lucky with that box."

The astonished little girl stared helplessly for a moment. "There is nothing in my box," she said.

"Not now," the woman said. "You just now used them. Would you like another grab-box? You have fifty cents left."

"Yes, I would." The little girl handed over her fifty cents and marched out just as she did before. And just the same, she tore into her new box. Outraged, she screamed, "THIS ONE IS TOO!" And she slapped her hand over her mouth, realizing that again she'd let her new four words go without so much as a thought.

***

The fire was dying down to black and the glow of orange embers. I was reading the *Theaetetus* mainly because it bored me, having Socrates compare his method to midwifery, an affront to midwives everywhere, but there was of course something amusingly instructive in his description of his interrogation, and so my first reason for reading it, namely to find some needed sleep, was rudely subverted. Sally was nodding gently toward some dream as her hands pretended to knit. But then she sat up.

"What is that noise?" she asked.

"What noise?"

"That thumping. At least there was a thumping."

"Houses make noises. In fact, all houses make noises. Was it from the basement?"

"I don't know."

"But you heard something, a noise?"

"I believe I did."

"You believe you did?"

"I did."

"Which one? You believe or you did?"

"I did."

"Houses settle, and they make noise. Was it a house-settling noise you heard?"

"It could have been."

"Whatever, you found the noise unsettling."

Whether the noise actually unsettled Sally Lovely, I can't say. I wondered if the house ever did make settling sounds, and whether it is was more or less settled after making them.

"Ishmael, do you believe in god?"

"Of course I do. Don't you."

"I don't know."

"You don't know if there's a god, or you don't know if you believe in him."

"Or her."

"So, you do believe there's a god."

"Why do you believe there's a god?"

"Because I believe in evil. I know there is evil in this world. I believe that I exist, and so I believe that god exists, a stupid argument, but mine. I'm an incomplete being at best, and god is that completion. So, in a way god's existence depends on my own. But the existence of the rest of world, the physical world and everyone else, well, that requires that god exist."

"You've thought this through, I see."

"At night, when the house is making its settling sounds. I grow blind. Hands! Stretch out before me that I may yet grope my way. Is it night?"

"What's that all about?"

"The whale."

* * *

There is a time for atonement, and it is the hour after midnight. At one. Atone at one. At onement. There will be perpetual leveling of all things at one, at once atoned. The flesh of sentiment will be stripped base at one, leaving little more than a skeleton. I can hear the bleating of sheep and the barking of greyhounds in the distance, but no such animals reside on this mountain. They must be the animals Art counts to find sleep. The dogs race in circles to find circles within circles. The sheep, wretched beasts, wait for the falling of the poleax to split open their craniums and their memories. Bubble and squeak. Sleep, that sweet retreat; I watch as he snores a little, tied up as he is, troubled in there, silver duct tape against his forehead. He smells of his own shit and piss and somehow I don't mind. They are earthy smells, these smells of living waste, bear dung and scummy pond water, elk droppings and cave drippings, death and blood and death and blood. His nails, fingers, and toes, are bloody, bloody as if wanting to chew them is the same as chewing them. Each finger is beastly dead. Each toe a lame whisper.

✳✳✳

Socrates was just a Sophist who didn't like Sophists. Easy enough to say, and saying it expresses little but a silly disdain for Socrates that I really don't have. Knowledge and virtue are one and the same. Now, that's saying something, I suppose. Of course that's what they said when they brought him that final cocktail; I imagine it in a split coconut with an umbrella and a straw. Me, I live on a mountain without an oracle, no sage to climb toward or to which to turn. Flycatchers are audacious little birds, but terrible witnesses to things they have seen. Water is never new. Language is an immoral universe. You should see 'em come round me of a Saturday night. If only we did have forms of utterance. Such is life, such is life—the bitter and sweet. And an unexamined life?

✳✳✳

And how does Ishmael Kidder click into the culture that is his? As a matter of fact, he does not. Not to play to cliché, though the temptation is not so much great as the pit is exceptionally wide, and say that he is a square peg in a round hole, but rather he is a round peg too wide for the round hole assigned him by whatever assigning powers there are. Perhaps his feet are too enormous. Perhaps it is his head, pumpkin-shaped and solid. Perhaps the deeds of his home government are repulsive and, therefore, instructive, two responses that are unacceptable, understandable, and hardly unpredictable. Ishmael Kidder respects, has come to respect his culture's chosen method of genocide, so slowly cooked, so slowly wrought as to have it appear benign, no slashing machetes, no gas chambers, no ovens, and never in the name of hate (no, never in anything so honest as *hate*), but in the pursuit of security (national), in the pursuit of that religion called *democracy,* of freedom supposedly for others, for all, the freedom we all know, the freedom that allows Ishmael Kidder to stand witness with no recourse but to go along with it all, like decent Germans standing by and watching the parade in 1939. Because at whom will he point, if he chooses to point, what will his complaint sound like, as no *one* is pulling the trigger, no one is swinging the blade, flipping the switch, turning the valve? Lessons are not lost on Ishmael Kidder. Revenge is a sweet but messy, imprecise but sating weapon. But it's okay, Ishmael Kidder thinks, his problems live at home, his problems live in his basement, his country, tears of thee, sweet land of the killing tree, but all that is forgotten, look away, look away, all of that is behind us, him in that hazy blur of AMERICAN history. America knows how genocide works; it works quietly, dumbly, but sophisticatedly in the way that it recognizes, approbates that mere life is not the painted target. Don't count the dead. The dead can walk. The dead walk with no language. The dead walk with no knowledge of their own destruction. The dead dance and play and frolic and trot off into the night to expire as tools, implements, weapons themselves, vague and imprecise, to *protect* freedom, the freedom of the rest of the walking, talkless dead.

∗∗∗

Only God could love you for yourself and not your yellow hair.

∗∗∗

There were only two full-length mirrors in the JCPenney store in Taos. I quickly purchased them both. They were of inferior quality, framed by cheap plastic made to look like cheap wood. I found myself being asked why I was buying two mirrors by the curious clerk, an extremely tall woman with masculine hands and a girlish face framed by an impossible helmet of hair.

"Why do you need two?" she asked.

"An experiment," I said.

She taped more paper around the floor model for which there was no box. The other one would be waiting for me in the back at the loading dock. "What kind of experiment?"

"I'm interested in various angles of incidence and refraction," I lied to her, leaning an elbow onto the counter. I then went on, "Do you know what the Venus effect is?"

"No."

"You see, there are these old paintings, usually of Venus, a famous one is by a guy named Velasquez, but anyway the painting could be of anyone. Anyway again, Venus is looking in a mirror, but her eyes are focused, concentered, if you will, on the person viewing the painting, not on her own face."

"I don't get it." Her voice had a truckish quality.

"If I can see you in a mirror, then you can see me. Can we agree on that? Well, if Venus is looking at herself, then her eyes should not be fixed on the person looking at the painting."

"Okay." She didn't want to talk anymore. The truckish quality was replaced by one of, not annoyance, or boredom, but of a hushed, tight-lipped, subdued alarm.

"Mirrors work that way," I said. "You can't conceal yourself in a mirror. Did you know that? Your reflection exists in and of itself, is a thing itself. It might depend on your presence, but it is not a part of you. It's a thing in this world, yet you can't touch it and you can't find it and it has no depth, none at all."

I left the poor woman disturbed, frightened, and ever-so pleased that I and my mirrors and my reflection, angles of refraction and incidence and Venus effect were gone.

I then went to the drugstore and bought the largest hand mirrors they had.

When the clerk there asked me what I needed all those mirrors for, I told him that I was vain and left it at that.

With the four mirrors from my house, the twelve mirrors from the drugstore, and the two big ones from JCPenney, I had eighteen mirrors. Light splashed and flashed everywhere as I dealt with them. I stood them, nailed them, and taped them around my work in the basement. I arranged them so that my subject could find his face no matter where he looked, and then I removed the hood from his head. He appeared startled by his reflection.

"When I hurt you, and I will," I said, my voice smooth

chocolate, "I want you to see all these other people and wonder which one of you is feeling the pain, which of you is feeling the pain more, less, which of you is only watching and feeling nothing." Since I had the mirrors configured to offer him reflections of himself and reflections of his reflection I could not see him in any of the mirrors, my understanding of the Venus effect, and therefore it was only faith that allowed me to posit and believe that his reflections actually existed. If I tilted a mirror so that I could see his face, then he would be able to see me and I didn't want to be there for him. I wanted him to have the company of infinite incidence and refraction, unending repetition, the forever drip drip drip of his own image. "Tell me a story," I said. "Tell me a story of a cheerless and disconsolate and pathetic childhood, tell me of your beatings and abuse and debasement, tell me who shoved a swollen dick up your sorry little ass. Make me cry. Make me cry."

***

Plato was fond of likely stories.

***

All flesh stowed, the basement secured, the house locked, I drove myself down the mountain and to Taos Pueblo. I paid to park and walked with the other tourists across the little bridge over Taos Creek toward the falling-down clay buildings. Watched a man there in sandals and socks, standing beside his wife in sandals and socks, as he steadied and pointed his camera at a craggy brown-faced Native man. The brown man corrected his posture on the wall on which he sat and stared at the lens. Once clicked, the Native man held out his hand, palm skyward. One pair of sandals regarded the other. I think he wants money, from the wife, he wants money. Pocket fumbling, the man wonders aloud, how much does one pay an Indian for his picture, and he settles on slapping a five into the brown man's hand, but the hand remains positioned palm-up, the five-dollar bill defying the steady breeze and adhering to the Native man's skin. The Native man's face was stoic and unmoving, his old craggy cratered face was so unchanging and wooden that it was a parody of itself and so finally quite expressive, in the way of a carnival mask. Another five and a one landed in the brown hand, then it closed. He regarded all four sandals and all four socks and said that the initial five would have been enough. You white people, the brown head shook, you must learn patience. He paused, looked at the sky, at his money. In his best Native voice, you white people must learn that guilt has a fixed price; it is not negotiable. Of course he didn't really say that, and it's not even clear to me that his eyes said it. In fact, I'm quite certain that if I had stepped in to supply those words he wouldn't have understood them at all, but they were there, in the air, in the creek.

***

Yes, it seems we have found the scoundrel and how do you like that old-fashioned, muddle-headed, and out-of-place euphemism for monster-who-killed-your-daughter we think he is the one the one who brutalized and murdered your little girl in that little park where the little boys played with their dog the breed of which we failed to take note where the narrow ditch leads to the wider canal led there then on that day yes it seems we have him the man who did this that horrible crime but what can we say because we cannot kill him hold him keep him lock him up throw away the key because he is the man the monster but he might not be the man the scoundrel how do you like that word that euphemism and we will keep looking scouring the ground and your child's underwear for evidence fibers hairs bits of mud the track of a boot blood saliva semen DNA and you will of course call us give us a ring if your daughter turns up won't you because we have the man had the man who murdered your child.

* * *

Aristotle believed there was a god. Enough said.

all knowing
true
unthwartable
eternal
all powerful
all loving

                         deaf
                         uncaring
                         disoriented
                         clumsy
                         mean-spirited
                         almost real

* * *

***

Glug, glug, glug. Give us another drink.

***

How I loved being a family. If could have been like Joyce marching across the field of Waterloo, wife and kids and hamper full of picnic, I would have been, just like that but adjusted for a later time. During one picnic, at a state park on the rugged coast not far from San Luis Obispo, I sat on the beach with Charlotte and in stony silence we watched six-year-old Lane play in the surf. The child would chase the ocean away only to have it turn back and bite her ankles, at which point she would run away.

I could here recount the bromidic, but all-too-telling details of the conversation, but I will not. It is sufficient to say that we talked, but failed to converse, said nothing to each other, but said oh so much. That neither of us was listening was precisely and decidedly what we heard. That neither of us was actually there, present, dramatically drove home the reality that we were all too much there, that our missing the point was in fact the point on which we were both helplessly impaled.

* * *

Every word is a symptom.
Every line holds the entire picture.
Every *every* is a lie waiting to happen.

* * *

And so it is that you should be left here on this life-drained, unremarkable corner of Los Angeles Street and Winston Street. I could have placed you deep in the Mojave, but here you are instead, at the bottom of this short hill, a concrete river to your east. Life-soggy cardboard huts and steaming-sad stacks of human flesh and bone, sleeping off this drug or that drug, crazed and lost, your neighbors in their houses. Small work that you are, you would disappear in the vast expanse of sky in the desert, but here . . . Here you share the confined, limited, but nonetheless vast wall, and even I don't fully comprehend this deployment of distance and scale. All I know is that in this great hall, this endless museum of only ordinary things, there is nothing ordinary, and so neither will you be—ordinary.

I'll let you out on this rock of a corner, and here is a bright shiny quarter so that your paper cup will not be empty. This will be your home sweet homeless, and you may find your way out if you can. Few do. But if you do crawl from this, the real frontier, the last frontier, the American frontier, you can, will remember the unwheeled baggage that I have given you. Drag it with you proudly, with a sure, august air, nameless one. Listen to my unwavering voice, always hear my baritone. The man beside you, the one with the blackened nails, the man who hears voices different from the one in your head, he will not hurt you, he will not harm you. He is too terribly weakened from exposure to the elements, reduced and faded from what drugs he can scrounge, from what drops of booze he can squeeze from the street. He used to have a family, this man. He used to have a job, this man. He used to have a god, this man. And you used to have me.

***

It turns out that pseudonymity is not only a herniation from family and social origins, but a rupture from artistic ones as well. My alter ego, or as I liked to refer to her, my alto ego, was in way over my head. She lit my candle at both ends and scratched my monetary itch. What she wrote offended me because I apparently wasn't offended by it, my sadness being, finally, that she had talent, talent in a world of her making and artistic comfort while I was painfully out of stride with how I might have wanted to *be,* artistically. Perhaps I didn't really want to *be,* artistically or any other way for that matter. The whole contemplation and business of being was confusing to me anyway, never a chosen condition, never a condition that could be abandoned, it being that case that the dead were bad and unreliable witnesses at best to what effect death had on their being. I had become Descartes' candle wax. Even if one gives in, accepts Platonic determinism, one doesn't have to kneel at the alter and like it.

(An aside: Not that mention of my father need be mentioned, he used to say that in this country, most things are black and white, mostly the latter.)

Unfamiliar, exceptional, and odd placements have their place, so to speak, and so I continue here with the troublesome, ever-cropping-up problem of naming, that is more like *being* than, say, tennis, conversation, or murder, but probably more like murder than tennis or conversation.

What manner of being have I achieved by adopting, not only the name of, but the peculiar artistic sense and sensibility of Estelle Gilliam? The name is a mere construction, my construction certainly, and serves with both referential transparency and tergiversation. That performative act of naming was a little like taking my own life, a painful admission, oddly, that does not suggest madness, as does the disclosure or averment that I am in fact sharing this life with the entity Estelle Gilliam. I accept that it is only the name that haunts me. But what comes with a name?

***

Lane's goldfish, named Goldie, was not quite floating on his orange-and-white mottled side, but he was close enough to it, close enough that veterinary attention would merely have been cosmetic. Lane stared at the world of her fish on her bedside table, the orange glow of the Cinderella lamp behind it, with a kind of illusive indifference in her brown eyes. Her sharper-than-mine five-year-old mind asked, "Do people eat goldfish?"

I told her they did not, though I remembered stories of lily-white fraternity boys swallowing them live and wiggling in keg-crazed hazing parties.

"So, he's going to die?"

"I'm afraid so?"

"Why?"

"All animals die. Some live longer than others, but all of them die," I told her.

"No, I mean why are you afraid?"

It took me a couple of beats to catch up. "'I'm afraid so' is just a figure of speech, an expression, just a way of saying that a thing is going to happen, and we can't do anything about it."

"I might have overfed Goldie." It was not so much a confession as a statement of fact.

"Maybe. Maybe we all did." We stared at the sick fish awhile longer, and then I picked up the bowl, the sides cool against my palms. "Well, I guess I'll take Goldie into the backyard and bury him. Do you want to come?"

She shook her head.

"You're just going to stay in here?"

"I'm afraid so."

***

Form mea, salverfornation is knot a splice of comforit, howlnever gooed that peace might fell, but a palace of shafety, containtment, a bliss, wither physicycle, emulsional or intellectrical, that is fray of exurnal vices and a couplet of internailed ones as swell. Saternation, it turins out, is a caple of map-folds aweigh from sirenitude. Soiledwaytion myheight keep you alivid, but it won't make you happy about it.

***

I will call it *belle noiseuse*, this work of mine. You are my masterpiece. How does that strike you? I will continue to work on you everyday, nudging clay here, tempering hue there, chipping at a corner, changing tense, altering key. In my mind, somewhere in this sick thing I call a mind, I have a picture of my goal, a model of my ideal. You are not my phoenix and neither, sadly for you, is your destruction.

> *What are you looking for?*
> *The pudding.*
> *The pudding?*
> *That's where I left the proof.*
> *The proof is in the pudding?*
> *You said it, I didn't.*
> *What proof do you have that the proof is in the pudding?*
> *I'll tell you when we find the pudding.*

Killing you will not be my last stroke on this canvas. My destruction of you, dear W., dear Art, dear Frenhofer, must finally be a fiction, a thing I approach, like Zeno to the far wall,

like the arrow to its target, the asymptote to the line, a nearing
to perfection never reached.

＊＊＊

> I might not, if I could;
> I should not, if I might;
> Yet if I should I would;
> And, shoulding, I should quite.

＊＊＊

Sheriff: I don't see why you just don't park yourself up there
and shoot them when they come.
Me: It is my water.
Sheriff: That's what I'm talking about. Water is like gold
here. Nobody would blame you if you shot somebody
trying to steal gold out of your house.
Me: Hey, you're supposed to be the law.
Sheriff: And?
Me: Bucky, it sounds to me as if you're encouraging me to
break a few laws.
Sheriff: There's the law and there's the law. There might be a
law against it, but that doesn't mean you can't do it. The
law is just words after all.
Me: That scares me.
Sheriff: It should. It's the American way.

＊＊＊

Each and every time I speak or act in this ever-thickening thing
I call a life, for lack of a better, more precise term, I am *doing*

something, I am performing (as much I hate that word), and the sum of all of these performances are in fact my so-called life, completely uninterrupted, since it's a given that either no thing is completely interrupted or everything is, as there is nothing that stops me from considering even the things that promise to distract me from some particular range of thought or direction of thought or action, and so my life, so-called, is a singular complex action or deed or even thought that I perform from the time I am born until the time I die or stop living, whichever comes first. It is one thing, one indivisible thing, peculiar and unique. I am not simply one being, if that is true, but I am certainly only one performance, one complex single action that is my life, an illusion of many performances, but really only one, compound and complete, without pause, without recess, without hesitation, even when I am indeed hesitating, somehow a given thought forming the integral whole, but what is that thought? What is that thought?

***

"Shan't."

***

What is a self-evident characteristic? What is not defined only in retrospect? This I ask myself and I ask you to ask yourself, dear victim, sweet W., sweet Reggie, sweet focus.

If he could he would walk long-legged and solo across the troubling space of this room, a cameraman, secret and personal behind him, tracing him a history, flashing him a purpose, shadowing him and telling him where he is and where he's been. He would wander into the kitchen he has not seen and find moderately priced champagne in the refrigerator, pop it open and drink, notice the burned stars and stripes on the floor. The red light on the camera would blink, but not the secret cameraman. He never blinks. He never winks. His eyes are wide open. The private and secret camera would hold the frame steady, move to provide frame, let him know where to stand, let him mark the frame, and as he might drink the sparkling wine he would see that there are no stars outside, no lights inside, only the blinking red, only the signal to the frame-marking, the frame-making, only a perplexing clue to one extra, secret sphinxlike presence, a mysterious finger on the recording trigger, hair-triggered and ready. Reggie would be free, free to walk his long-legged yellow-haired swagger-of-freedom walk across the floor and out the door to the safety of a world that hates him, that he hates, a world that smells his foul barn-floor breath and is in turn sniffed by him. His fingers twitch while he watches innocent little girl-children in the park, his fingers wet with his own focus, his own juice, his husky breath stealing air from the rest of the world, waiting for a bat to the back of his head again, waiting for his absolution, his deliverance, his sweet dismissal, his death-dick-sucking vindication in the form of a bat to the back of his head, his name knocked loose, his name rolling out of the frame. Blink. Blink. Blink.

***

"I'm taking you off this blasted mountain to dinner." Said Sally, sweet Sally.

"That's fine. Just let me get my food together."

"Please just eat the restaurant food."

"I don't trust the restaurant food. I don't want the restaurant food." And I want to tell her the joke about the two old ladies who are sitting in a deli, but I don't tell her, but the joke is that these old ladies, good blue-haired friends, ancient lunch buddies, are sitting in this deli and the food is brought out to them and one is having a pastrami on marble rye and the meat is piled eight inches high and the sauerkraut is an inch thick and there is Russian dressing visible all around the edges and the other woman, who is still clutching her purse, is looking at corned beef on pumpernickel, similarly proportioned, but without the sauerkraut or dressing and they each have on their plates pickles the size of machetes and one says to the other, 'The bread is so terribly dry,' and the second says, 'The pickle is far too sweet,' and back and forth they go with complaints about the stale sauce and the too-thinly cut meat and the wilted salad and finally the first says, 'And the portions, they're just so small.'

"If you ask very politely, they might just let you go into the kitchen and watch them as they prepare the food."

"I don't need or want to do that. It's just that I don't know them. I don't know where they've been or where the food was before it got to them."

"The same is true of the grocery market."

"Then you can see what a problem I have. I trust eggs and oranges and anything that comes in its own package."

"Things can be injected into eggs. There's nothing that can't be tampered with."

"One has to have a little faith."

***

I call the president of my country (here, because I can, because this is my world and you're welcome to it, if not welcome in it) (and someplace in some other note I said for you to fuck off or fuck yourself), I call him the Marquis Façade. But that implies something behind the face, some substance, whether shallow or deep, behind the mask, but something behind the mask, and it simply is not clear that there is. The façade is not a layer, not a mask, not a veneer, concealment, or pretense, but what you get. When you've touched its front, you've touched its back. How does one not build a straw man when his opposition is made of straw? How can there be Manichean thinking when there is only one column of attributes? And one wonders what tarts are made of. Pepper mostly. Maybe treacle.

"What we expected to achieve was never realistic given the timetable or what unfolded on the ground. We are in a process of absorbing the factors on the situation we're in and shedding the unreality that dominated in the beginning."

Winner, Best American positional statement: *They're lying, too.*

> The King was sitting in a tree,
>   Thinking with all his might:
> He thought with all his facilities
>   To cast the gloom as bright—
> And this was odd, because he knew
>   Already that he was right.
>
> His mistress played the keys nearby,
>   Because she thought the sun

Might break through the clouds
        When the pillaging was done—
"It's quite unsporting of them," said she,
        "To die and spoil the fun."

The sands were white and full of oil,
        The blood on our hands was dry.
You could see no smoke, because
        No smoke did fill the sky:
No crying babies disturbed the troops—
        There were no babies to cry.

* * *

Who is this man?
He is a beggar.
I am a beggar.
I am Saint Martin. You are cold. I will give you my coat.
He does not want your coat.
I do not want your coat.
But you are cold and I will give it to you. I will be cold
and you will be warm.
He does not want your coat.
I do not want your coat.
What do you want, beggar?
He wants you to either fuck him or kill him.
I want, no, I need you to either fuck me or kill me.
Fuck you or kill you?
He says yes.
Yes.

I will give him my coat.

He says you do not love him as yourself. He says you are no saint.

You are no saint.

But this is a warm coat.

He says the coat is made to be shared. He says you are healthy and will not mind the cold. He says you are selfish.

You are no saint.

I am trying to make a sacrifice here.

He says you are not.

Fuck me or kill me.

But it's such a nice coat.

He says—

You stay out of this. This is a nice coat, beggar.

It's not even cold out.

Please take the coat. I've come all this way.

Nope, I want to be fucked or killed.

Listen, I really need you to take the coat. I'm begging you.

I don't want the bloody coat.

Please, do it for me. Take the coat. It would mean so much.

* * *

For Plato and perhaps all of the sandaled and toga-clad ancients, the problem of philosophy was finally a conciliation between the worlds of appearance and being. The problem is that *being* is considered perfection, pure being is so considered and assessed, but I can tell them, the ancients, that being, even pure being, even pure being of state, even pure being of conception is always less than the sum of that being's appearances, always less that the sum of that being's shadows flashed against some cave's walls, always less than what is left after the distillation of all the preconceptions and conceptions and presumptions and assumptions and illusions and delusions and lost dreams and found betrayals and discovered absences, and so I am left with this recourse to intuitive social disentanglement or at least some kind of abandonment of a notion of density of feelings. Maybe, maybe, maybe. Every word is a symptom.

* * *

My dissatisfaction, my irritation, a strange but true designation, with my life did not descend upon me like some cliché fog, though in the middle of it I kept waiting for it to lift—like some cliché fog. It started like a rumor. I didn't believe it at first, then, in human fashion, I ignored it, then I couldn't ignore it and I denied it. I told Charlotte, well, I tried to tell her, but I didn't make much of an impression, perhaps because I made little sense, perhaps because I lacked the conviction of belief myself. Months later, she asked about my distance, my blankness, my remoteness, my inanition, and I reminded her of my earlier admission and so she asked if I was unhappy with her and I answered honestly, not always a good idea, saying that I didn't know. It turned out that "I don't know" is the wrong answer to "Is our relationship in trouble?" Then, to complicate the cliché I may or may not have had an affair. I imagined that I had had one, though my description to friends of the encounter led them to tell me that I had not. I was convinced because I was unwilling to tell my wife. As I look back, I realize that there was no love there, however intense the feelings, but I kept coming around to the idea that my dismissal of it, because of the mere but significant absence of sexual contact, was mere rationalization. My wife became convinced that there was another woman. I was conflicted. There was no other woman, and there was another woman. I had not been unfaithful, and yet I had failed to remain faithful. I did not love another, but I could not say that my love for her was unchanged. I had not fucked another, but I had imagined fucking another. I was repeatedly left with the true, but unsatisfying, and, apparently, increasingly infuriating reply of "I don't know."

A friend, a self-assured woman, suggested that I might as well go out and have sex with "the other woman" since it would be assumed that I had anyway, since I was just as guilty in some eyes as if I had anyhow, since I couldn't seem to tell the difference anywise. But I couldn't and I shouldn't and I wouldn't and didn't quite simply because I was too afraid of it all, perhaps not a manly position but it was mine. I was afraid of hurting Charlotte, afraid of hurting myself, afraid of hurting the woman who had stupidly become fond of me, afraid of Charlotte's rage, and afraid of my lurking inability to stop once I started. I was afraid I might actually like it and afraid that I, sadly, wouldn't. All of that rings and rang then like feeble and rueful vanity, as if I really in fact had the consequential power to *cause* pain, as if it were my choice to activate such a relationship.

***

What is a stable identity? You are not the man you were when we met, not the same man you were before I first tied you up to that plank. You are not the same man who raped and murdered my little girl. Even though you are, you are not. You were the sinner, but now you are the punished, someone new altogether. The question is, are you the same man? Am I to place individuality in some notion of unity of matter or in some idea of consistency of form? If I replace this house completely, one board at a time, will I have a new house at the end or the same house with new lumber? You have all new skin and hair from when you were a child, your blood is new, the cells that make up your organs have been replaced, but you're still you, aren't you? Maybe it all comes back to names, but people change their names, get called different things, forget their names. So, it's not how you appear and it's not what you're made of and it's not what you're called. So, what is it? I'll tell you what I think. I think that we never change. It may seem that you have changed temporally, spatially, physically, but you have not. You're not moving ahead through time, not walking through space, not growing and shedding and renewing and graying, but instead dimensions are passing over you like waves. Dimension after dimension, like waves in the ocean. No time is passing. No time has ever passed. No time will pass or come. We have been, are, and will be here, in this moment, forever, you and I. We will be forever here in this space, you and I. Although I change your name when I please, you are, in this moment, in this place, consistently, one thing and let's say that is *my guest*. That, my friend, will be your identity. Who are you again?

* * *

Zen the ra'd shehook the hijr und so eye howled din the kahf. So many steeps, a mirage, ma'arijingle the waqihahahahaha.

* * *

"Lane will not stop asking, she wants to know where you are at night."

"Tell her I'm in my bed asleep."

"She wants to know why you don't live with her anymore, if you're still related."

"She'll understand it later."

"She's asking me now."

"I'll talk to her."

"When?"

"Tonight. I'll talk to her tonight. I've got to get this manuscript mailed off and then I'll come right over."

"She cries."

"I don't know what to say. I can't fix it over the phone. I'll talk to her."

"She cries almost every night."

It just had to be true. It was the word "almost" that nailed it. Had she been lying to punish me, she would have said that Lane cried every night, but she said "almost every night." A thing like that just has to be true.

* * *

***

I'll be going upstairs now to take care of the visitors. You should pray that I take care of them, and that they don't turn the tables, so to speak. Because where would you be without me? Remember, you're not real of course, but only the sort of thing in my dream. If I just end this sleeping, well, where would that leave you? Pray that I remain asleep. Pray that I don't awake. The two are not the same. Do you hear them up there? Ditto and Ditto-Ditto? Tweedledo and Tweedledone? Pray that they do not wake me. I know that, while you are down here with nothing to do but think, you end up pondering all sorts of things, among them whether you are or are not. You've probably derived your own sort of *cogito*. I fear, therefore I am. But you don't suppose those are real fears, do you? Creak, creak on the board above. I must go take care of business. *Deformis est,* I realize, but this is what we do.

***

***

the first swing was left to right backhanded handle held with firm thumb on the bottom of the grip point toward shoulder blade facing away from elbow from above my head down through the moonlit dining room slicing air then skin through muscle ligaments tendons cartilage bone through short-lived surprisingly shrill scream shout spraying coughing blood spatter across the table the rug the wall into my already stinging eyes arms flopping up into the next upward twist swing body weight pushing both cut deep between elbows and wrists hands fingers failing to find open throat river wide like a mouth sing screaming mouth while the tearing eyes face of the second man gape open to receive accept the third blow all in a matter of troubling seconds tic tic no more than ten no less than four honed light-glint machete stuck into his forehead like an ax in a stump like a sight gag his scream in the darkness with yellow moonlight through the clean windows eyes crossed taking in the blade seeing watching the blade split vision reeling falling backward without a deliberate step raised arm or hand not dead but will die shock killing all movement but for quivering twitching fingers squeezing the air twitching legs fluttering crossed clownish twitching eyes behind a diaphanous veil of blood curtain of blood wall of blood behind chop chop blood slash slice dead dead oh what a relief it is and dead is dead and there's no taking back no going back no giving back and dead is dead is gone is dead is bloody bloody dead

***

Language is said to have at least five functions:
    1) to impart information
    2) to express attitude or emotion

3) to conduct, alter, or influence the actions of others

4) to create artistic effect

5) to maintain social bonds

But I dare say there are others:

6) to manipulate the feelings of others

7) to cover previous language abuses

8) to cover previous emotional inadequacies

9) to fill a void

10) to cause pain

***

He was in the trunk of my car. He was a very heavy man, so I imagined that his weight might improve my traction, like sacks of salt or cement in the bed of a pickup keeping my tires close to the hot asphalt, close to the spinning of the planet, keeping me from fishtailing out of control on the heat of it. I had a real, living, possibly human being in my trunk. I had bound him up tight with 3M duct tape after hitting the back of his inebriated juiced-up potted and unsuspecting head with a hardwood tire bat that I'd purchased at a truck stop. Once, I'd struck him only once, having remembered a line from a movie or a book. "The first one's free," was the line. I didn't know what the second strike might cost me and to whom the price might be paid, but I needed him alive so that I could have his life, possess his life, take his life, needed to have him see his life stolen. He was stashed in my roomy carpeted trunk, his mouth duct-taped shut, tearing at the corners of his sick-dry lips. I drove just a bit faster than the limit (their limit) so as to not seem suspicious or worthy of attention, as nothing in this culture is more suspicious that adherence to the law. Interstate 10 rolled east, away from Los Angeles.

***

The blue house on the corner is synonymous with *the house on the corner is blue. She makes everything beautiful* is not synonymous with *everything beautiful she makes.*

***

Food for thought is no substitute for the real thing. For ex-simple, one p-knut bitter and kelly sandwhich well knit yelled the auntilogistical argument. A walt on the wield sighed and a wryed in a cart oon the hideway true the swamp.

Where does Daddy think you are? I don't know, Daddy. Where do you think I am? Does Daddy miss you? Yes, Daddy, you do. It's raining and I am crawling across a sweet eider carpet, a mat of leaves under my knees. Can you smell the sweet compost, Daddy? Where is Daddy looking for you? I don't know, Daddy, but you might try beneath the shrubs, where the dog is sniffing. I'm in the swamp. Pogo is not here with me.

The swamp is wet. The swamp is dark and wide and in places deep.

Shaggy hairy-backed snaggle-toothed leg-dragging scale-faced lip-turned red-eyed pot-bellied long-toenailed cranially crooked dung-odored toe-jammed short-toed hammer-toed lock-jawed lock-kneed carrion-breathed scratchy-tongued unwashed unkempt unleashed unlearned unlinked unlovely unmeaning unmoored unclothed unboxed uncorked unbuttoned uncaged unanchored unapt unbuckled unsavory unruly ungovernable intractable and refractory was the monster in the swamp, the thing in the swamp.

Where does Daddy think you are?

Why does Daddy think you're silent?

Why does Daddy think you cry?

***

I was forty when I left Charlotte, a nice round number forty, divisible by two, four, five, eight, ten, twenty, and of course one and itself. Had I waited a year my age would have been a prime number, but as it was it was merely nicely even. With forty came a gnawing dissatisfaction with life and an additional disappointment that I was like all those men whom I laughed at when they went through their so-called midlife crises. The problem with the crisis was that it didn't come like a crisis, like some big event, but daily, like weather, like meals, like work, like plumbing.

There was a terrible snowstorm in Denver, or so the news reported in great white detail to us. Charlotte and I were sitting in the den, reading, the news harmlessly yakking on the screen in front of us. When the report of the snowstorm came on, I closely attended to it thinking that I wanted to be there, maybe stationed along the side of the highway someplace helping fearful motorists who wanted only to get home to their families, put chains on their tires. I knew how to do that, put chains on tires. I thought I could do that for free or perhaps even charge people a couple of bucks. Regardless, I would put on their chains and see them off, watching the chains I had installed churn up the dirty ice and snow.

"What are you thinking?" Charlotte asked.

I didn't mention the chains. "I was thinking how great the weather is here."

"Another day in paradise," she said.

I laughed a seemingly inappropriate laugh, and she just looked at me.

"I'm going to make some tea. Do you want any?"

"Yeah, I'll have some tea."

She got up and left the room. The news broadcast was showing an aerial shot of cars stranded along the interstate highway, some turned sideways, some stuck at strange angles into drifts. I could be there, I thought, in one of those odd-angled cars, buried under a old quilt or wrapped up in one of those foil emergency blankets, trying to keep warm by eating a chocolate bar and rubbing my thighs with my gloved hands. Then I became heartsick as I realized that it wasn't that I wanted to be in white and snowy, frigid Colorado, but that I didn't want to be in chirpy, lightsome California. I didn't want to be in my house with a book open on my lap, with my wife making tea in the kitchen, with my familiar and irritating television making familiar and irritating noises in front of my propped-up, socked feet.

Charlotte returned with the tea. "I made you herbal. That way maybe you'll get some sleep."

"Thank you." I watched her set it down. "You know, we should call it a tea table. We don't drink coffee, so it doesn't make sense to call it a coffee table."

"Okay," she said.

"Tea table," I repeated.

She studied me for a few seconds. "What's on your mind?" she asked.

"Nothing."

"I saw that Natalie today." Charlotte tucked her legs up under her on the sofa. "You know, the mother of Lane's friend Becky, the one you think is hot."

"I didn't say that."

"Well, you do think that, don't you?"

"Just because you happen to think she's hot doesn't mean that I think that."

"Well, no. Don't you think she's attractive?"

I pulled my feet from the tea table and leaned onto the arm of the sofa to look at her. "What's this all about?"

"It's okay for you to think she's attractive. We're mature adult people."

"Thank you for your permission."

"Don't get defensive. Just tell me what you think."

"I think this is an ambush is what I think. Any conversation that has in it the disclaimer that we're adults is . . ."

"Come on, we're sophisticated people."

I looked at her eyes; they seemed playful. "Okay, I'll bite. Sure, I think Becky's mother is sexy."

Charlotte was silent, the playfulness in her eyes fading before mine.

"What?" I asked.

"I didn't say *sexy*," she said.

"Okay, beautiful."

"I didn't say that either."

***

Zeno believed that there was a confusing of physical magnitude with mathematical magnitude, that if you considered them the same, then his paradox was a real problem, depending on what one means by *real*. He actually posed no problem at all with his pair of ducks, Anaxagoras retorted by resorting to halving flesh because you can always cut what flesh we have, again. You never cut a thing down to nothing. There is never a final cut. Daily, I slice away at my love for my daughter, at my guilt for surviving, at my resolve for revenge and slice away at merely myself, and it remains painfully obvious that I'm all still here, always big enough to be cut a million more times. And so, no matter how small I become I remain infinitely, miserably, painfully, laughably, eternally, and interminably large.

***

Lovelustlessness, indeference, twill ever be abell to generhate suckficient power to schlow down and *flinger dintently* clover an oddject, to whold and sculpt everich detale and perticular in it, howlever mynewt. Only glove is capsable of being aschew-thetically preductive; lonely in the corerelation with the gloved is foolness of the manlyfold plossible.

***

My wife didn't ask for the pain I gave her and this is something from which I might never recover, whatever recovery comes to. And what a sad self-serving and self-pitying load of crap that is (this sentence to be read parenthetically). She thought, no doubt with good and just reason since she was stationed better than anyone else to read such a thing, that she was happy, happiness being an elusive thing or state at best, a thing that at least one friend told me was not something to search for and certainly not something to pursue. There was a lot of talk, and we know what good talk is, unless of course you have no concern with standards of truth, talk offered to minimize what I had done by examining my own suffering and comparing it to the suffering of others, culminating with the insipid notion that the one who leaves hurts more than the one who is left. That was of course complete and utter bullshit and, worse, it was a bit of winging the beater. It was not a competition to see who could suffer more profound pain. If I had hurt more, if I could imagine such a stupid and useless measurement in the first place, and which I'm sure I did not, what relief could that or the knowledge of that have offered me? If it worked that way, I'd have marched around with a crown of thorns on my head or wrapped around my dick. But that's been done. To my credit, and I take this credit because there are so few available to me, I never considered wearing that crown. Besides, a crown is simply a noose that doesn't fit.

***

Up through the strangely thick brush. The filthy men didn't know I was there. My dam was below me, I on the hill. To their credit they had not put their lives to chance by attempting to blow up my structure. They came, and not noiselessly, disturbing a deer that ran past me without a pause. I pumped my shotgun, letting that dramatic sound hang in the air until they paused to notice it, their ankles cold wet in the water, their hands filled with stones to divert the flow. I called down to them, and I could feel their veins chill. I called out, "Wrong night, wrong night!"

They looked for me on the hillside.

"If I were you I would run!" I said.

I fired into the air away from them. The sound might as well have been thunder for the way it shook the forest. Sleeping birds took flight, and for a few seconds the trees were alive.

The men ran into each other and fell over.

"Run!" I called. "Run like chickens!" I pumped and fired into the air again.

They had lost any and all orientation and struggled to maintain balance.

"Make chicken sounds!" I shouted.

One of them did, I think.

"Run!" I shouted.

They faded into the thin darkness. One of them screamed back, "Fuck you!" from deep in the brush. He sounded near tears. He said it again.

I couldn't help myself and it felt bad, but I let out a good laugh that might as well have been thunder.

* * *

This passage, this one here, illustrates one of the difficulties of my silent (what I mean by silent is anyone's guess) monologue (what bullshit that is) that the reader (however you constitute or recognize yourself, if you chose to be one, the other, or both) must create the scene and identify the present actors (as if mere puppets are capable of action, as if actors imply action) from sheer implication (or maybe imputation), from some hint or insinuation of evidence (that fleeting concept that is always mere perception) left tethered to the fraying ends of lines (think of actors or fish), as it were (is). I may playfully or not parody my own mannerisms, but who is to say? Could I, could I be a *bloody doubledyed ruffian?* My aching knuckles are red bloody and sore. My beakers and dishes are stained. My lab is busy. Flakes of skin cover my floor.

***

For Epicurus, would that I could commit, every sensation is devoid of reason and incapable of memory: it is neither self-caused nor does it have an external cause or cause anything externally. More importantly (and more importantly for me because it is beautiful in its way, neither is there anything that can refute sensations or convict them of error. All sensations are equally valid. So, if what is in the bowl in front of you tastes like pudding, but smells like bat shit, you cannot over-ride one sense with the other. You simply must accept the fact that you like the taste of bat shit. And where is the other side of that parentheses?

***

The sheild eyed been playinplain sightin the front yardlot of her mother's cobbyhouse, just as she had a thousand times. There head nil doubt been a coolingentle breeze and perchaps a wisp of cloud had drifted in froth of the sun. Charredlots had seen her there, leaning on the candlebars her bicyclic, and adjust minutes lather, the bicycle was there alone, laid on the wasland of grassgreen between the slithewalk and the curb, that strip of land which killed have belunged to Charlotte or the city where I'll tell about the child, all you want to hear and well you know her and you'll die when you hear and tuck up your sleeves and loosen your talk tapes, and I'll take you to the place where the child had never laid her bicycle before.

***

From a nail on the wall I took the machete, eighteen inches tip to hilt, rust red rubber-handled, molded to my callused palm from years of garden use, and sharpened all night one night when the basement was empty and quiet and lonely and waiting. But that evening my head was not empty, my head was full of dreams, vivid stirring dreams of filling my basement with the restive, breathing body of the evil that now stands tilted and tape-tied down there to my fir plank. The beveled blade was sharpened that long-ago night, and now it was ripe and ready to use, prepared to respond to the sounds up those stairs, to the sounds of the unfortunate drug dealers from the valley who had come to kill me maybe, maybe only to try to scare me, maybe only to hurt me a little, to teach me a lesson, to save face. However, into my quiet house they came, came, came

swing, swing, swing, slash, slash, slash, blood, blood, scream, scream, blood, done, done, done

Well, almost done, as very little is really completed. Things change. People change. Completion is change, and as such it meets with protestation. Heraclitus peeks up from behind that ever-shifting, maybe burning, bush and tells us that nothing is permanent but change. But of course no change is permanent, and so permanence is never complete. And so we are forever what we are, changes or no, once an alcoholic, always an alcoholic, once a pedophile, always a pedophile, once a child always a child, and once dead, always dead. I'm being some-what literal here, aren't I? You've come to expect more of the abstract from me, but, you know, I find the abstract somehow cruel, somehow selfish and mean-spirited. Why can't a tree be a tree? Why can't cold-blooded murder be cold-blooded mur-der? Well, almost done

slash, swing, kiss, fuck, kill

***

Lane was outside playing with the neighbor's cocker spaniel, a nice enough, overweight blond dog that "wouldn't hurt a fly," when suddenly the dog snapped and bit her face. She was just four at the time, and it happened so very fast; she was play-ing with a dog that she had played with dozens of times, I was standing not three feet from her, kneeling even, my face nearly level with her face and the dog's, and the dog seemed to move as slowly and predictably as ever. Then the dog lashed out, without a sound, quicker than my reaction, quicker than my child's recoil, and caught her on the chin, splitting it open and drawing blood. I didn't punch or kick out at the dog as I thought to do an hour later, when a helpless anger set in like language, as I sat in the emergency room with its filthy floor, while a communicatively deficient doctor sutured the wound shut. It was not a bad wound, the doctor said as much, didn't even really require sutures or staples, but he was doing it any-way, not a bad wound at all, but all I could imagine was what if the dog had struck a little higher or lower, with a little or a lot more force, what if his tooth had caught her eye or throat? What if the hard bone of the dog's head had slammed into her temple? I couldn't stop thinking and I couldn't stop shaking and yet I couldn't shake the image of a greater harm and the image made me sick. I hated myself for not stopping the bite, for being so so slow, so trusting, so late. Because it could have been worse, a lot worse, and I wouldn't have been able to stop that attack either. It could have been terrible and I wouldn't have been able, capable, quick enough to stop the dog and what kind of father was I to let my little girl play with that dog, though she and I trusted the animal, though she had played with him dozens dozens dozens of times, what kind of man was I to assume that any animal was safe around my child? The imaged possibility of a decidedly worse outcome became irrefutable and so tangible and therefore the worse outcome became reality for me.

And contrast the following scene with the previous.

Imagine that it has all been set up for you, that I am not the lazy fuck that I am. Charlotte, Lane, and I have made the drive from Los Angeles to Bryce Canyon in Utah, a bit of chill in the air, both outside and inside the car, but basically all is well. The landscape has inspired awe and closeness, and the child's laughter has brought the two parents around, closer. Imagine that you have suffered through the transitional scene that moves you from the car to the edge of the short trail that leads to the observation area where many people are standing, pointing, speaking English, German, and French. Lane has wandered ahead to snap a photograph. I walk with Lane. She is five. Lane points to the red rocks near us and remarks on how she likes the color. She asks what that color might be called. I tell her it might be rust or maybe sienna. She likes the word *sienna*. She tells me she likes red.

"Red is my favorite color," she said. There was a four-foot-high chain-link fence to separate tourists from falling. Lane became afraid. I could feel it. She stared at the edge and gripped my hand more tightly. I could feel her little palm grow moist against mine.

I knelt beside her and whispered that everything was just fine. "What is it, honey?" None of us had known about this fear of heights. How could we have known? It was certain that Lane hadn't known about her phobia.

I leaned forward to take a peek over the cliff, and she pulled my hand.

Charlotte came back to us, camera dangling from her wrist. "What's the matter?"

"I think we have a problem with heights," I said.

"Are you okay, baby?" Charlotte asked, stroking the child's hair, pulling it from her face.

Lane reached for and clutched Charlotte's hand. Charlotte looked at me. "She's really scared."

Seeing that she now had her mother's hand, I again moved to the edge to look over into the canyon.

"No," Lane said.

"I'm just going to take a little peek," I said and smiled at her. And then I moved a step closer. One step.

Lane screamed and started to cry.

I came back to her, and she refused my hand. I didn't move again to see into the canyon. I told my child I was sorry. I felt anger at myself. Anger because the step I took, that step toward the edge, that seemingly innocent step toward the source of her fear, was a step I was taking only for myself.

***

Plato insisted on these three levels of knowing a thing. Well, sort of. He stated that there are three classes of objects through which knowledge about reality

How are you to construe, interpret this interruption? Given the nature of my notes thus far, is this interruption an interruption at all, or is it an illustration, or an exemplification of sorts, of a method? As with any method there are constraints, boundaries, rules, curbs, and checks, or it would be no method at all or, at least, a very poor method indeed that might not be followed or employed. How are we to construe the constraints? Are the constraints attempting to check the limits of meanings, interpretations (because the two are not the same thing), inferences, or do the constraints, by virtue of merely being and being merely what they are, mean something themselves? And if so, what? More importantly, though, why? We're always about the business of what a thing means. I want to know why a thing means. Why do I mean by that? A much more complex and perplexing question

                                    must come. Put another way, for things that exist, there are three layers of bullshit that we must penetrate—and then a fourth and a fifth (afterthoughts). They are, first, a name; second, a description; third, an image; fourth and fifth, the knowledge of the thing and the thing itself. Afterthoughts. And what about the reality of the *image?* What about the knowledge of the *name?* What about the name of the image?

Does my victim, dear victim, dear, have a name? A description? An image?

***

***

"'Give me your evidence,' said the king.
'Shan't!' said the cook.'"

***

And so my novels of romance, though they are hardly romantic, of untamed unbridled unmanageable lust and fervid, even indelicate, animal attraction (as if there were another kind) were what they were, no more, no less, pretending nothing and offering no apology, and as I wrote them, write them, to change tense in midstream or flow or river or current, I wonder who gets to say what makes them what they are and what they can contain and reveal and how many features of the thing as it is can be changed before if is no longer the thing that it was and why can't I pause in the sky, the god that I am, during some steamy removal of some hat or cape or bra and simply tell the lost and lonely woman who is reading my formulaic, predictable, though albeit well-written, novel that she should be attending to the fact that her beloved country is torturing people and breaking its own highly held laws and substituting capitalism for democracy as a system of government and raping the world, and how can I do this without seeming like a raving political pundit paid by political tools to promote some political position instead of simply being a man who is ashamed of his country and trying to offer a moral truth and do so without sounding naïve, which I no doubt am, but does that make me wrong? And it's all rather silly, isn't it? Because cynical as we are, jaded as we are, I sound naïve. Regardless of all truth, I am quite naïve to write this. But I am happily (and oh read this word ironically if you do nothing else) naïve.

***

It could be either/or and and or either or and or either or or and and, but either way it was either Kierkegaard and/or Freud where in dreams either/or equals and. Or else? Oh, my god, I've boiled my watch.

But what if I posit here that my mission is solely literary?

That I am out to undermine and erode a particular literary genre. Yak, yak, blather blather, clunk. What if I leave it at that? What if I, my character, am a man infected, soaked with the disease of the genre I profess to practice? Am I a rogue Palmerín or Lancelot? May I here casually brush aside all claim to the reality, so to speak, of my so-called and weakly convenient so-called story? And what if this is all a ruse, cleverly supplied to cover my daring and yet evil and yet simple deeds, to cover my trail, my ass?

This is my sweet and delicious alibi. And what an alibi it is. I simply say that none of this is real. This is not blood you see on my hands, under my fingernails. This network of implications is nothing more than mirrors and strings and a little smoke, blood and judgment, good or bad, so well mingled, and perhaps discursive, but only in your imagination, as I tell you also that I have eaten smooth creatures still living.

***

"If only my consciousness had a flowing stream." This to Sally as she drove us up the mountain at dusk.

"If I've told you once, I've told you a zillion-ca-billion times, don't think about art. Fuck art. Just write."

After some desert and some sage and some stunted trees, the shadows of birds, the slithering of snakes, the humming of beetles' wings, a slight shift in the wind, a whiff of standing water, a glimmer off a metal roof, I caught her glancing over at me.

"What is it?" I asked.

"You need somebody up here with you, to keep you company," she said.

"If I were happy I'd need someone. I'd need someone to share it with. But this grief, this grief can take care of itself."

***

The scariest, most horrifying, unnerving monsters lie in wait in deep darkness, in black shadows, offscreen, in the wings, in caliginosity. I am a strange and curious construction, naïve, driven (in the sense of fated or duty-bound, but hardly coerced and certainly not merely giving in to an urge), and, above all else, sovereign and supreme in my soothing, convenient, almost sweet contradictions, so sentimental in my stories and precise in my mission as I adhere to every motive and device of those I choose to mock. The most alarming, most terrifying monsters are self-conscious, self-aware, knowing full well the evil and depravity of their actions. We are not the socio- or psychopaths, for they have an excuse, a plea to damage even if they don't plead their own cases. But I, this strange, bizarre, unruly, and contrary construction, know full well the evil and sickness of my activity and view it ironically, and not sardonically, holding it ever close as sincere, if crusty, artistic expression, a tenuously veiled representation of my time, place, and people, and so my license is current; I am free to create, as it were. Pass the rib-spreader, if you please, and make the little child tell me, please, her name, please, why with a name like that you could be any shape, almost, and tell me again that she, and therefore I, can't be put back together again.

Every morning I wake up healthy. As it is for all monsters, this is a bitter, amaroidal disappointment. I am dead and gone or at least well on my way to dead, if not quite gone, and I cannot imagine a more horrid interruption to my journey than this relentless good health I find myself in every sunup. That flat mirror, that picture of another world where I am flat and without dimension is a land of infinite and boundless health it seems. When I stare at that reflection, I am not staring at myself. I am staring at a reflection. A needling distinction that is worthy of note if not rote.

***

The best way to deal with reasonable objections to your course of action is to keep your course of action completely to yourself and insist to yourself that any objection you might generate on your own is unreasonable. This is hard for us humans though, vanity being such a strong force.

Category Mistake:

Two boys, twelve and six years of age, sit on either side of their father at the counter in a diner. The waitress, a nice apple-faced woman with an bountiful waist, wipes the surface clean in front of them. She looks at the twelve-year-old and asks what he would like?

He looks behind her into the pastry case. "I'll have a piece of that damn pie," the older boy says.

The response to this comment is abrupt and decided as the father slaps the lad on the back of the skull and sends him lurching forward, chest to counter.

The surprised and rattled waitress, after taking a few seconds to compose herself, turns to the younger boy. "And what would you like, little feller?"

The six-year-old looks over at his brother and then at the

waitress and says, "Well, you can bet your sweet ass I don't want any of that damn pie."

***

I'm glad, so clad, you could join me on this faustive occasion. But whay kant I rejoyce on this ascension of my naughter into the clouds of heavydom? Can a scream be articulate?

***

We slice, cut, rive, cleave, rend, split, tear open the entire body from the anus to the chin. Find a fold of skin on the belly and grab it between your thumb and forefinger, roll it between your fingers, then carefully puncture, pop, pierce the skin. Avoid perforating the gut. Then simply, plainly, easily, honestly slit the body open all the way up to the throat and down to the tailbone. When you find the sternum and the pelvis, just, merely, simply (always simply) cut down to the bone with your knife. When you come to the testicles, don't cut them off. Simply, plainly, easily, honestly, cut the skin between the testicles and leave one testicle attached to either side. Then carve, divide, chiv, cleave, slice down through the hams to separate, divide, dissociate the buttocks from each other. It's important that you cut straight down. Once you've apportioned, parted the hams, take your sharp knife and score out the anus. Now you've got him slit from stem to stern. Once this has been accomplished, achieved, realized, locate your meat saw. Cleave through the sternum until the rib cage is open. Then saw through the pelvic bone. Do not perforate the bladder. If you cut it, you'll spray urine over some of the best meat on the hindquarters. Keep the saw blade parallel to the bone and cut carefully. Take up the knife again. Cut the windpipe just under the chin and grab hold. Separate the smooth muscle tissue holding the entrails from the carcass. Slice this tissue while you pull on the windpipe; the entire gutpile will come easily free, will roll out. Be certain to completely remove the colon and the bladder, which can sometimes hang up on the pelvic bone. This is a source of bacteria and also heat, so it's very important to remove all of the entrails. The elk is field-dressed.

***

"You're not embarrassed?" Sally asked.

I was pulling containers of my meal out of my bag. It was set on the floor, and I was leaning over for the elk chili when the waiter came. He had seen me before, but the familiarity did not breed friendliness. I nodded to him.

He nodded back, but his eyes said, "You, again."

"I need a big plate and a bowl," I said.

"We serve food here, not dinnerware," he said.

"Fine," I said and I glanced at the menu. I searched and found the most expensive item. "I'll have the Kobe steak and the blanket-wrapped asparagus, but hold the bacon. In fact, hold the steak and asparagus, and bring me the plate. Now, for the soup. Sally, what soup shouldn't I have?"

"I'll bring the bowl," the waiter said. He took Sally's order of beet and goat-cheese salad and roasted free-range chicken, and then he walked away.

"You're impossible," Sally said.

"Oh, I'm perfectly possible. He doesn't care. He'll get his big tip, and he'll have me to complain about when he goes home to his wife whom he met in college. She has a gap between her front teeth and does needlepoint when she comes home from the veterinarian's office where she cleans kennels. She never seems to get the smell of disinfectant off her nails."

"And how do you know all of that?"

"I made it up."

"Anyway, Jack Nicholson already used that bit in *Five Easy Pieces* with a chicken-salad sandwich."

"Well, it was the character Jack played, and it was egg salad, and you'll notice that I actually got my way."

"I do wish you'd use your powers for good and finish this damn novel."

"I've got plenty of money, more money than I need."

"Well, I don't," Sally said.

"Take some of mine."

"As much I'd like to, it doesn't work that way."

"You're like everybody else in this country, hung up on silly rules." Just then a young Native couple walked into the restaurant with their lively little girl. She was three, perhaps four, and her hair was done up in long braids. Her dark eyes were bright and eager to take in the restaurant.

Sally caught me staring.

"You'll never get over it, I know, but is it any better?"

"It is what it is," I said.

"Have you heard from Charlotte?"

I shook my head. Rather, he shook his head as I now shift to third person (because I can) to convey a sense of distance and at once, ironically (as all things are ironic), to offer this intrusion that makes me and so you even closer to the narration and so to the story and so to the pain. He shook his head, glancing only briefly again at the little girl. Her father was getting her situated in a booster seat, his large hands wrapping nearly all the way around her.

"Do you want to talk about it?" Sally asked.

"What is there to talk about, Sally?" he said. He peeled the plastic cover from the rectangular plastic container and sniffed the elk chili. "I can say a thousand times that my daughter is dead, and nothing will change."

"You could talk about how you feel."

"About how I feel?" Ishmael Kidder aka Estelle Gilliam shook his head. "Any idiot with a pulse knows how I feel, how I must feel, how I will feel, and I don't ever wish to feel anything else. Talk about what? Myself? Poor, poor me?"

"I understand."

He looked around for the waiter, then back at Sally. "This is where I'm supposed to snap at you and say how could you possibly understand. Well, I'm not so much of a cliché, and of course you do understand. Who wouldn't understand my grief and sadness and loss? I would be one of those self-indulgent, self-involved masters of avoidance who say to well-meaning and clearheaded people that they don't understand." Then he became quiet, because he had talked more than he would have liked, because he was making his rather understanding friend uncomfortable, and because the waiter had arrived with Sally's food and his plate.

***

I held the razor (actually a hunter's antler knife with a scrimshawed handle and an angry-looking gut hook on the end) to the man's naked throat. He had little hairs there, and I watched the light from the bare bulbs glint off the polished blade that

I had spent the better part of an evening sharpening. I held it unswerving, firmly and ardently there, steadier than I thought I could or might. He tried not to breathe, or to not breathe, but breathing really isn't a choice, is it? Sadly. His Adam's apple moved toward the blade with the action of his swallowing, and his hairs stood straighter. I had imagined his bumpy, pimply throat and this blade so many times, so many times. Somehow I knew his throat, as all throats are pretty much alike, though I hadn't imagined the hairs. The hairs were a surprise. His hands were tightly secured behind his back and to the chair and I paused to consider the word "secure."

But I would not spill his blood. I wouldn't touch the metal to his flesh, his meat, though the blade was close enough that ions were transferred, that the current of his nerves ever so slightly magnetized the polished steel, and so he felt the edge, the edge of everything and everywhere, the spirit of the blade interfering with his synapses, crossing his thoughts and his body's hapless, useless, hopeless, and wasted communications.

"Don't bother counting sheep to find sleep," I said. "Count your fingers. Count them over and over. Count them and remember them. Memorize them. Memorize your fingers."

***

My friend, the sheriff, the fat and upstanding, noble constable, Bucky Paz, is crushing the cushion of the armchair in the living room of my house. He has the beige crumbs of something that leaves beige crumbs in his mustache. He is a pleasantly obese man who laughs easily and sometimes too loudly if he knows you, and sometimes if he doesn't. He is drinking from the steaming mug of coffee I have given him. He blows on it.

"I'd go up there, camp out and shoot them when they showed," he says.

"Why don't take your gear out there along with some sandwiches and camp out?"

"I never go out camping. I need my bathroom and cable television."

"You don't even own a television."

"So, I go up there and simply lie in wait and then shoot them when they show up."

"Yep."

"And then what happens after that? You would come and arrest me and take me off to prison. They're only diverting the water for their pot. What could I use, the thirst defense?"

"Those druggy assholes down in the valley are doing more than growing pot. They're making meth and if I catch them, I'll shoot them myself. If you shoot them, I might be looking the other way. You never know."

"It's the 'never know' part that bothers me."

He laughs that laugh of his, and the whole house seems to shake with it. Then the house seems to shake against it, one wall, then another. "What was that?"

"What was what?"

"A thumping."

"Oh, that. I've been meaning to tell you. I've got a man tied up in my basement."

Bucky laughs bigger than before. "You kill me, you beat everything," he says.

"No, really, there is a man in my basement." *And here the philosophical paramedics hover over me, fanning me with the pages of Heidegger maybe, and one is saying that I've had a nasty bite, that I've come down with a case of parataxis, and another is say-*

ing that I simply refused to lie, was perhaps incapable of it, and that in itself was evidence of something wrong, and yet another, a skinny, ill-looking woman said that perhaps my use of the truth was a narrative device meant to make absurd a truth that had not even suggested availability and so was a sign of a level of linguistic sophistication that the other paraphilosophics were not granting me.

* * *

The notion *life* is an almost annoying intellection. The term *life is* an obvious abstraction and not very useful, as we cannot think about everything at once. So when we talk about *life* we are in fact trying to talk about everything while in fact we are talking about nothing. O Mouse, do you know the way out of this pool? And so it is the same with all talk of god, another glorious and useless abstraction. We cannot know what god is like because god is just so terribly *awesome*, and so god is beyond our meager understanding and our limited and struggling imagination even. So, all talk of glory-be-high-god is necessarily, axiomatically, ineluctably nonsensical, and you can tell the mythical bully I said so. We know nothing of god, so how can we speak of god. I know nothing about zero-gravity negative-booster inhibitors, and anything I say about them will be nonsense. Oh, I can hear the wheels turning in your pathetic god-believing god-washed god-fearing god-happy thought-rinsed ganglia you call brains. You're thinking: but you just referred to, spoke of zero-gravity negative-booster inhibitors and so at least, at the very least, their mention entails some kind of existence. Even if I made them up. And I don't buy it.

But wait. It seems I could be wrong:

Imagine a zero-gravity negative-booster inhibitor that which none greater can be conceived.

***

Lane's eighth birthday was the first of her birthdays after my divorce from her mother. It came just three months after my leaving. I lay quietly on my bed, staring out at the behemoth bank buildings looming over me in downtown Los Angeles. It never got very dark in my flat. There was never any fear that I might stub my toe in the night. I could see the walls and my desk and the photo of my little girl and her mother that I kept on my dresser. I wanted to cry, not so much because I was missing my daughter on her birthday (I would in fact see her in the morning), and not because I had any creeping thought that perhaps I should not have left my wife, but because I hated so much the pain I had caused my wife. I could see her looking at places in the house we had shared and picturing me, wanting to hate me, and maybe succeeding to some degree, but mainly feeling hurt and confusion, and I could all too well see the way her face would become even prettier seconds before weeping would twist it. I felt so awful, lying there in that room that would never be dark enough to conceal me, felt unworthy, perhaps worthless, looking for something worth feeling, for something defined enough to feel. I had for some time entertained the notion of returning to Charlotte, wanted so much to be her hero, as if she would even consider taking me back, but I wanted to be that man, to swallow the fact that I was unhappy and by habit of pretending, in that fashion of Aristotle, achieve some comparable state, but I couldn't do that. I had in fact tried it many times before and had failed miserably, perhaps I had even made Charlotte sadder by my efforts, perhaps she was considering me pathetic for them. I would never know and could never know, and it would never matter anyway. Aristotle believed that the definition of a thing should state its essence. I wondered how Charlotte might define me.

***

Ishmael \bas-terd\ *n* [Heb] **1.** Someone that is spurious, irregular, inferior, or of questionable origin **2. a :** an offensive or disagreeable person—used generally as a term of warning **b :** a non-feeling, despicable creature who leaves with no good reason and wrings your heart in his fist while pretending to be compassionate and understanding—**Ishmael-ly** adj

***

there was a time when I respected the place of art and tried to protect it from the world that called itself real, but I never tried to keep the dirt of the real off my own pages even though my pages were soiled with commercial considerations, even though my pages sought no meaning beyond their surfaces, even though my pages made me sick to my artistic (a pretense that I actually had one) stomach, I tried to protect them from the world and the politics of the world and the deceit of the world and the shame that was my country teaching the world to slide bamboo under fingernails to slowly slice scrotum from left to right or right to left whichever way the text reads or doesn't read my country 'tis of the thee I sting my country right or wrong love it or leave it and it's a good thing because it's always wrong but it has taught me to torture and so I torture and seek definite descriptions precise definitions clear marks of identity or identities defined by other identities that might or might not exist my country love it or leave it salute the flag but thank it for the luminous example that I use as I wield this obsessively honed knife to this throat and watch these beads of perspiration form on this face and hairy neck while I wonder if Man X is Man Y or exactly identical to him in every way down to the place in space that he inhabits and isn't it always the XY of it all . . .

A question mark someplace???

***

My mountain would ask me every morning at sunrise what the present demanded of the past, and I would tell it I did not know. I think my words were, "I do not know." When I no longer exist, a child's or philosopher's way of saying when I'm dead, will I belong to what present there is? Which is a way of wondering if I will belong to the future that will outlive me, as the present that once was a future has outlived my daughter, who lived as nothing but a promise of the future, with so little past and such a fleeting, vaporous present. Her present is still, even without her presence, and no future, complete for me without my knowledge that she will be there, in my thoughts, in my dreams, in my every breath.

The mountain was asking me again as I turned to find Sally asking me if I wanted coffee.

She would be leaving later that morning, and she was satisfied, I believe, that I was all right.

"No coffee for me," I told her. "I'm glad that you found it. I like it when people make themselves at home."

"Are you happy writing these books?" she asked.

I looked at her face and she looked older now and it wasn't just the terry-cloth robe and the absence of makeup. "Where's this coming from?"

"I know that you hate these novels, and I was just wondering if you might like to write something else."

"Thank you," I said.

"Thank me for what?"

"For the question," I told her. "I really don't know if I'm unhappy writing this shit. I know it's shit, but what the hell. Maybe anything I'd write would come out as shit. I don't know. But thanks for the question."

She sipped her coffee, blew on it. "You've been a good friend all these years," she said. She looked off at the sunrise. "I'd like to be one to you now."

"Okay, Sally. I'd say you're doing a pretty good job." I looked at the sunrise with her, then toward a gathering of clouds in the west. "It's going to rain this afternoon."

"Is there anything you need to say? I know it sounds weird, but that's what I'm asking."

"It doesn't sound weird. There probably is something I need to say to somebody, but hell if I know what it is."

"You seem lonely out here."

"I'm anything but that. I don't even know what loneliness amounts to. Besides, I need to be out here."

"Well, I'd better pack," she said.

"I suppose that would be a good thing?"

"Are you sleeping okay? Can I send you anything?"

"Sometimes and no."

***

It might well be that insinuation is the lifeblood of fiction or perhaps more to the point, the finger of its fate. The logic of the story is enough, always a predicative, if distinguishable from propositional, logic that at least sings with a familiar voice, a voice that is learned in childhood, a voice that can lie all day and night, and still it is a true voice. Premises of arguments need not be right or wrong, they need only be in the correct key. It is not necessary to prove that the premises are inconsistent with the negation of a story, only that there is dissonance; that is enough to prove validity, if not truth. We are humans; our standards are low.

***

And so the evening came on as every evening comes on, with
the broken-down, fatigued, and irretrievable day bending and
breaking into small, insignificant, indiscernible pieces, with the
babbling, gasps, squealing, and reverberations of the streets
collecting into a familiar drone, with all the bright and silvery promise that had come with the morning finally, quietly agreeing merely to return tomorrow. I watched from the
corner, sitting in my car, as the man who had been called a
suspect, labeled a prime suspect by the police, who had been
designated as *guilty as sin* by the portly district attorney with
the weak chin, walked out and onto the not-so-busy but free
street. He was not in any way an exceptional-looking person,
didn't look exceptionally evil, foul, depraved, or dangerous or
degenerate, but he did look exceptionally guilty and blame-
worthy, this I could see from half a block away. He walked his
uneven, not-quite-a-limp stride, and then I was out of my car
following, through Chinatown and then south, circuitously,
as if he had no destination in mind, as if perhaps he had no
mind, to a bar on Fourth between Main and Spring, a place
with a door shaped like a keyhole. He was a large man, and all
I could imagine as I watched him hunched over the monkey-
piss beer he had scratched change together to buy was that
frame hunched over my fearful child, my terrified, lost, and
confused baby, and at that second he was guilty, without question, without doubt, without any appeal to a standard of guilt,
guiltier than anyone had ever been, guilty of rape and murder
and terror, and I was the cop and the judge and the jury and
the executioner and god, and god, was I filled with hatred,
sweet righteous hatred, at that moment, his lips white with

the foam of his beer, and it really wasn't hate at all because I really felt nothing, nothing at all, just cold, steady, unwavering and unswerving focus, benumbing bitter ice-cold resolve, and there he was and I was god, god was I god. I wondered at the medieval distinction between contrition and attrition and imagined myself one in the long line of corrupt, praetorian but infallible and divinely touched popes drawing on my boundless treasury of merit to exact proper penance. This man, this guilty man, would not feel sorrow for his loss of love of a god, a convenient myth or not, but he would feel sorrow, this I would see to, sorrow at least for the pain and suffering that he himself would experience. I would see to that.

***

anaphora
burlesque
quip
jibe
    anaphora
    reproach
    derision
    twist
anaphora
metonymy
synecdoche
conceit
    anaphora
    aposiopesis—shhhh
    asyndeton—no ands, ors, buts
    litote

Deceptions are telling not only about the deceiver, but also about the deceived, the values and perceptions of the deceived, and about the necessary relationship between the deceiver and the deceived. But all of this is obvious; you cannot be deceived unless there is something you really want to believe. You really want to believe that the old vase is valuable, that you are smarter than others, that the child is really yours, that there actually is a deity. The great deceiver understands that the deceived actually does all the work. If a deceiver wishes to calcify a person's acceptance of the deception, he need only suggest that what he has been selling is false. And of course the most devastating deception might be one where we become convinced that we have been deceived, that what we have thought was true really isn't true, and so we finally reject what is truth. Once the deception has been exposed, then we must distrust the new revelation of deception because we know we can be deceived, and since we now know that we can doubt the truth, that particular truth will never be as true again.

    Heraclitus and his river.

***

Meye slapping aweigh came afthere the turd thyme. I twas wyeth my naughtier and my swife had lift the howuse anglery. She callid me forum hear care, seecreaming at me. I knew what her driveling was licke when she was on the phony, when she was hoopset and I refussed to talk to her useless she pooled over. She screamed mores. I hung up. She called black and screamed more and then in mid-sen-tense-scream the phoneme vent blink or dread, but dead was suck a scarry word and is. She left me to lie to our daughter, telling her that her mother was okay, telling her that her mother was on her way home. I was terrified and helpless and I called the police and asked about accidents and I paced and lied to my daughter and grew angry and scared by turns. When she pulled into the drive I was too exhausted to be mad, and however much I was relieved that she was all right, I had to wonder if a little bit of me didn't want the drive to remain empty.

***

It is hard to be concerned with the center if you keep getting bogged down in the periphery. That much was clear. Well, a lot more and a lot less than that was clear, but clarity is what you make of it. I can't see the clarity for the trees. The room is cluttered with clarity. I'm tripping over it, slipping on it, losing it behind the refrigerator. There is more clarity than I can shake a stick at. Too much clarity for one room. Too much clarity for one person. Clarity out the yin-yang. Clarity that has never before been regarded. A tub full of clarity. A sky full of clarity. Clarity that glows in the dark. Clarity that beeps when I clap my hands. Clearly too much clarity. Clarity out the ass. A snowstorm of clarity. A fog of clarity settling on the hillside of clarity. Clarities colliding. Clarities expanding infinitely away from center of clarity. Clarities smushing together and making more clarity. Clarity pressing at the seams, popping rivets, bubbling over.

And yet . . .

***

He might have thought I was gay or simply an alcoholic like himself, but whatever, he seemed more than eager to have me accompany him to another bar where I would buy him more much-needed booze. His one beer had had no effect, and yet he eyed me only a couple of times with any kind of lucidity, but his look scared me. At least, I think he scared me, as his eyes had the quality for the briefest second of a mirror. This man was a criminal, a killer, a predator, a stalker of children, a dirty-penised slug from the underworld. Most importantly he was my killer, my dirty-penised slug, and I needed him. I walked him over to a restaurant called the Daily Grill (I imagined the menu covered in incriminating questions), an upscale yuppie hangout where I knew he'd feel lost and ill-at-ease and out of his element and would turn to me in his alcohol haze for bearings. We sat on stools at the bar and the man, who by now had told me that his name was Reggie, which was somehow short for Roger, which was somehow a nickname for William, twisted in his seat to spy on every woman in the place. I bought him cheap whisky and he drank it down, his throat opening like a circus act. The more he drank the more subdued and nervous he became, more aware of how out of place he was. We didn't really talk. We just sat there next to each other and watched the football game on the big-screen television.

"Tell me, buddy, you ever play football, I mean, on a team?" he asked.

"Never did."

"I did. In high school. I was a defensive end." He looked at his glass. "That was a long time ago. What about you?"

"Never did."

"Oh yeah, you told me that."

"You know, you don't look like a Reggie. Or a Roger. Or a William."

He laughed. "What do I look like?"

"Let me think about it."

He watched the screen for a while, then looked at a blond woman at the end of the bar. He then pushed his own blond hair off his face. "You know, you're all right."

"I like to think so."

Reggie got slurring sloppy lost-on-the-street-man-drunk and the pony-tailed slick-haired actor-want-to-be-bartender, who wasn't the least bit thrilled with Reggie when he had been more or less sober, gave me a dirty look.

"Call me a taxi," I said, and the boy-band bartender picked up the phone.

On the street, Reggie looked at me with puzzled dog's eyes and said, "Where are we going now?"

"Back to my car," I told him. "It's not far. We're just going to my car."

"Then where?"

"We're going to hell, Reggie."

***

From the formula of Ignatius Loyola the crazy fathers recited the horrors, the smells, the sights, the sounds, the sick and foul tastes of hell, and had I a soul, a sliver of a soul, an inkling of a soul, I would have vomited.

***

Why the old woman lived in a shoe I don't know. That it was not a sandal seemed clear enough to me. That she didn't know what to do with so many children I understood. But that's all I could ever remember of the rhyme. I wondered why she'd given birth to so many children and I wondered where was her husband and I wondered if the shoe had rooms and if the children wore shoes that looked like their house and if they did, did they live in them, their shoes, or did some other old women live in them, their shoes, with their children and I wondered again why was an old woman like that, who should have known better, having all those children anyway and where was the father? Fear was a cold wolfman too jived in a stew.

***

Here in topsy-turvydom a man can control his voice and words and yet make no sense and still have the senselessness of his utterances be true. He can stamp out and construct riddles round about and say that ideas smell like myrrh.

***

There was a dog. I trained the dog. It was part Border collie and part poodle and part something else. The dog was smart enough. It was a hyperactive animal. He was easy to train. He wanted something to do. Charlotte did not help with the training. Charlotte didn't follow through with commands. Charlotte complained about the dog. She complained about the dog's behavior. She complained about what the dog chewed. She complained about the way the dog smelled. She complained about where the dog peed. She complained that the dog did nothing she told it. The dog would stay when I told it to stay. It never stayed for Charlotte. The dog would sit for me. It would never sit for Charlotte. Charlotte decided the dog liked me better.

I argued that she needed to help train him. She did not help train the dog. She told me again that the dog liked me better. I told her I thought she was correct. That made her mad. The dog only understood short sentences and Charlotte spoke only in long ones, offering impossibly compound commands, never accepting that the dog not only wanted to obey her, but needed to obey, but of course didn't know what obeying her came to because he had no idea what she was talking about. *Come in here and sit down before I scream* was a poor command. As was, *Stay here while I think*. We gave the dog away.

***

Bringing it home, summing it up, nailing it down, and putting it in a nutshell, in a word, natural intelligence (would that it were natural) and a good memory are equally powerless to help a person who has no innate affinity for a subject. I wonder how many times Plato was slapped across his pudgy face? All who lack any natural aptitude for justice or some other nebulous moral principles, though they might be both intelligent and retentive in the study of some other matters, and all who have such an affinity but are stupid will never attain a true and true-hearted understanding of the most complete truth in regard to moral concepts. I fairly accept this and embrace it even; my hands tremble every time I walk past the not-so-sturdy door that leads down to my cellar. I'm not the least bit intrigued with the nature of the moral concepts that either drive me, or that I have somehow run afoul of. My actions have been, are, and will be merely actions, simply actions, like daisies and rocks on a hillside, notebooks and pencils on my desk, like things in this world. They will finally have been like food, sustaining and necessary, perhaps bad-tasting or sick-making, but passing, temporary, fugacious. Sometimes I think life's mission is the elimination of singular terms.

***

"What is he having?" this from a bulbous man at the table next to ours.

The waiter was caught off guard because he didn't want any of my food in the restaurant and because he in fact didn't know what I was having.

"It's elk stew," I told the man. "They don't serve it here, so I brought my own. I butchered the elk myself and grew most of the herbs."

"It smells really good," the man said.

"Spicy," I said.

"I'd like that," he said to the waiter.

"We don't have elk stew," the waiter said.

"You're a troublemaker," Sally said to me.

"Well, I know what I like. I'm paying thirty American dollars to rent a plate. I don't think they really mind. Besides, I'm what you call local color."

***

"roloc lacol llac uoy tahw m'I."

***

They crept in from the mountain night and they shouldn't have, they shouldn't have, but I understood that I had raised the stakes by firing on them up at the dam, albeit with shotgun shells filled with bird shot from well away, well enough away that the bb's fell like copper drizzle against their down vests, if finding them at all, but still I had frightened them and so they slithered into my house, into my home, to take care of business, as they might have said, to take care of business, two of them, dressed like night, high on their own dope perhaps but probably not, and I was deep in the basement when they came into my house, busy with my business, messy with my mess, duct tape on the walls, against skin, and there was their noise, above me in my house, creeping, creeping, slithering, more than the settling sounds of the walls, but the sounds of creatures, and I recalled the shuffling shuffles of little slippered feet, bunny-eared toes against the hard wood outside my door before I would hear the small voice ask for me, and so the sound now, though no shuffles at all, came to me with haunted familiarity, at least by the fact that it was the stirring of life in my house, while beneath it I was busy with staining my hands, and I had to put down my roll of tape, my can of water, and walk to the foot of the stairs where I paused and calculated and paused and finally walked up, pausing between my own creaks, squeaks, the cracks of my old bones, old bones that knew deep in them that it was the drug dealers from down mountain, there because I had frightened them and threatened their perception of their manhood, and I walked up to find them, in my house, in my home, I walked up to find them and to kill them, not because they were intruding, not because they were threatening my life, but because they were going to find me out, they were going to disturb me in my intimate business, the busy business in my basement with which I was so busily busy.

***

Thehair is a diffdefference beetwhine a diffiference and a daffyerential.

*　*　*

The loss of the doll was huge in the child's mind and so huge. Lane remembered having seen the doll last on the floor in her room. I hadn't moved it. Charlotte hadn't moved it. The cleaning woman had not yet made her weekly appearance. Lane's five-year-old eyes were open, dry, and confused. It was the absence of tears that let me know how serious was the matter. I knelt in front of her in her room and asked her exactly where the doll had been.

She pointed to a spot between her night table and the window. "She was right here."

"Okay. Well, let's think about it. Where would a dollie go?" My patronizing first attempt was met with the first tears. I shook off my clumsiness and my impulse to focus on guilt about that and directed my attention to the problem at hand. "Okay, okay," I said. "Where did you go after you saw her there?"

"I don't know."

"Did you go to the kitchen to find Mommy?"

Lane paused and considered the question. "I went to the bathroom."

"That's good, sweetie. That helps. That will be where we start. Come on." I led the way to bathroom, and we stood there dumbly staring at the empty tub and toilet.

"So what did you do in here?"

The child gave me a look that I might have expected from an older child, then let out a sigh and said, "I made pee. In the toilet and I flushed and went downstairs."

"Okay, downstairs we go." We turned to leave, and I noticed the hamper under the towel rack. "Was the hamper lid up or down when you came in?" I asked.

"I don't know." It sounded like a complaint. She was being defensive because she had been told to close the hamper. Truth was I often left it open. I lifted the lid of the hamper, and there was the doll. Sadly, however, Lane's attention was now on having left open the hamper. She left her doll, didn't even look to see it in the hamper, and stepped, head hung, out of the room and down the hall.

I took the doll and followed her. When she was on the stairs I went down to a knee and pretended to be pulling the toy from the corner. "Lane, here she is. I think she was hiding from you."

She smiled, not a huge smile, but one that made me relax, made me feel like a decent man.

"Is that a game she likes to play?" I asked.

"Not until now," she said. "Thank you, Daddy."

I sat on the top stair and watched her make her way down. I was struck by how much of getting anything right was accidental. Either I had clumsily made everything all right, or my daughter, with the genius that comes with the absence of vanity, had allowed me a way out, had allowed me to play father one more time.

"Hey," I called to her as she reached the bottom. "Does your doll have a name?"

"Yes," she said.

***

After Abu Ghraib (I know that this is no place for some cheap political trick, nor is it an appropriate forum for challenging my political foes, slight and stupid as they may be, but, hey, this is my fucking world and welcome to it), the CI-fucking-A reviewed itself, a move not unlike allowing convicted serial rapists to mete out their own punishments and choose their prison guards, but who else could review such dealings and workings and secret shit? They, the C-fucking-IA, *scrutinized* the agency's interrogation and detention practices at military-operated facilities and *other sites.* May I point out that *detention* implies the subsequent act of *release.* But I am thankful to the boys in red and blue ties and trench coats and bloody gloves and no doubt starched white undies. It's not that they invented the practice of waterboarding, holding a person submersed until he believes he is going to drown. After all, a number of interesting and smart women were punished in this way in Salem, Massachusetts, for clearly being interesting and smart and women and so did a number of rightly skeptical heathens and clumsy believers in Europe, but the CIA reminded the world and me of the forgotten method. We'll call it a classic, a golden oldie, a keeper.

***

And Haditha.

And Beiji.

What shame? What sweet instruction, nectareous education. What vindication. What convenient absolution. What a model. What an emblem. There are not many gods, but only one, my country screams, our god of love thy neighbor, one god and we simply, happily don't believe in him (because it is a *him*, you know).

Isn't that right, Jesus, sweet Jessie? Sweet son of the one and only gaaaaaaawd.

Whatever on Earth do you mean? These words from sweet, gentle Jesus, rock-swinging in his hammock swing, blue-eyed and blond.

Tell me again, Jessie, about the love thing. How's it work and how does it look? How are your hands?

Drink this wine, it is my blood.

So, you'll forgive anything. No matter what I do, all I have to do is say, I'm sorry.

I will, I will, instructions from my daddy, don't you know. Here, eat this bread, it is my flesh.

Surely, you can't forgive all things. What if I kill a fourteen-year-old child's parents and her five-year-old sister and then I rape and burn her body. Will you forgive me if I do that?

But I can and I will and I do.

Here, eat my penis.

What is it?

My penis.

***

Socrates, we are told, sought to release what was already in the mind of the person being questioned, and claimed therefore to have nothing positive to teach, that there was nothing he was transferring from his own intellect to another. In other words, he would wait until his victim realized that he had been in agreement with Socrates all along and just didn't know it. We call this an epiphany. Meanwhile, Socrates openly professed his own ignorance and was ostensibly appealing to others so that he might become wiser from their intellectual journeys. Meno accuses Socrates of being like the torpedo fish, of torpifying those who come near. I don't know what *torpifying* means and I don't care to look it up in my OED, because the answer is already in my mind.

✳✳✳

✳✳✳

After I left my wife I would lie awake at night and recall the way she would on occasion walk out to the drive to greet me as I rolled up. She would do a little excited dance and I could see that she loved me and I loved that she loved me. As I lay there I would feel not strange, but expectedly empty and lost and wonder what in the world I thought I was doing in that alien bed, alone, wonder how I could leave all those intimate inside jokes and secret pet names and reserved private gestures and then I wondered what it would have been for me to remain, to walk through those days hollow and unhappy, having her see me unhappy, having her hear me unhappy, having her realize that one of the reasons I was still there, besides that I still loved her, was that I was too weak, too wobbly and forceless to leave. To remain would have been cruel and finally toxic, because how else could she have read my unhappiness except as a failing of her own, a fading of my interest and attraction, a diminishment of her beauty or charms and, finally, worth. Lying there, my eyes focused on a bad spot on the ceiling, I would recall her voice and her smells and the way her bare feet landed heavy on the hardwood of the bedroom floor and I would experience a sense of profound sadness, grief, much guilt, loss, perhaps even great loss, but not regret.

* * *

How is my puppy? What a sweet wittle puppy. What a whimpering wittle puppy. How is my puppy? Can you see the clock from here? The one on the tower, so far away over there. You might need these field glasses. You might need an unobstructed view. You might be a good puppy yet. What do the rednecks say? Oh yeah, oh yeah, that dog won't hunt. Wittle pup. A scratch behind the ear, wittle pup. A scratch on the belly. So excited, you've wet the floor.

As odd as it might seem, my named one, my troll, my puppy, my art was is in good health, or shall we call it verdure. It is hard to mind much when one's health is good. I speak of his physical well-being, as if mental and physical soundness can be separated, are to be separated, our always, you might say faithfully, being Cartesians; we can't help it. *I have something on my mind.* There is *I* and there is *my mind* and somehow they are not the same thing. If they were I could supplant one for the other. *I have something on I (or me).* Or *my mind has something on my mind.* You see, our language is hard-wired (as much as anything human is hard-wired) for us to think this way. But it gets peculiar with *I'm of two minds on that subject.* W., your health is good; let's leave it at that. Who's to say anyway whether my treatment of him, if I may refer to you as if you're not here, in the third person, as it were, has left him better or worse off inside his head, a bad and unpopulated neighborhood at best, not interesting enough to be a puzzle, not complicated enough to truly be frightening.

He's not so different from the monsters we call troops and send off to war. Not a popular thing to say, but they are trained killers. Just because they're our young men doesn't make them good young men, not down to a man, not every single man. After all, they have chosen to carry guns. Not one thought or imagined he would be joining to protect democracy. That insipid and predictable rhetoric comes later, when convenient. The thick-necked, ruddy-complexioned, sideline-redneck recruiter doesn't mention that. He mentions travel.

He mentions money. He mentions training. He mentions the stiff spiffy uniform, foreign adventure, ubiquitous sexual opportunity, and attainable situations for the abuse of physical advantage and power, but he doesn't sell it all by saying, "Don't you want to defend democracy?" But, troll-dog, how have I gotten here on this subject? I wish I had a soldier, a troop, to teach me what I'm doing wrong, to teach me why it is you remain in fine fettle. But I guess I want you in sound condition, your heart beating strongly, so that I might cause it to skip a bit, a tick, a beat, your mind reasoning reasonably well, given your limitations, because the proper experience of fear requires the capacity to calculate the coming results or causatum, to close with a dubious alliterative punctuation to the matter. I need you proper, so to speak, and sound so that I might tear you apart, as I do myself, daily. And you can see what it's done for me.

Things, the notion *things* being one I love, will go on quietly enough. We will have hazy yellow mornings, of which you will be unaware. I will tell you about them, in detail sometimes, and about the auburn sunsets as well. It is by a streak of fortune that you fell into my orbit, into my so-called life and I into yours, all bad but a streak nonetheless.

Here's the thing, troll-puppy, god hates us both.

***

. . . For both our oars, with little skill.
By little arms are plied,
While little hands make vain pretence
Our wanderings to guide . . .

***

"Yes," I said to the detective, "that's my daughter. She's all there." I didn't know why I added that, except that somewhere in my mind I imagined the police still out there looking for some piece of her. I was no doubt saying it to myself so that I would in fact stop searching. But of course I wouldn't; I would scan the eyes of every child I would meet, seeking some bit of my little girl. And I wondered what a bit of my little girl might be. A finger? An ear? But of course I didn't think that. It would be some look, the way a child might move, a smell maybe. I would sense it, seek it out, and find, every time, disappointment. It would be a nothing, a vapor, that line that can't be crossed, a rain shadow. She was all there, and there all of her will remain.

Here we are now as we've been before, confounded by the window and angry at the door. All of the books and all the words and the pictures and the mirrored walls will never shed light, will never yield sounds that will make any sense once we've spent all our rounds. The whole nine yards they called it back then, when women were women and men were still men, when the world went to war with clear villains true and Columbus was justified for crossing the blue. And idiocy reigns where idiocy lives and the henchmen love war for all that it gives and slogans abound in sweet Alabam while each daily life is revealed as a sham. To go on would be silly, but silly or not, the daily is all that's left, it's all that I've got.

***

Ouch is perhaps the only learned sentence. A child in learning and saying *ouch* is saying, "I am hurt," or "That hurts," or "That will hurt," or "Pay attention to me." Blah, blah, blah. *Cabinet* could work as a sentence in an imagined scene, as when I am crawling for my much-needed medicine and have only the strength to say, "Cabinet," which is the same as "My meds are in the cabinet." I would argue, and I suppose I am, that children never learn words, they learn where words should be. Blah, blah, blah. They don't learn *cup*, they learn that Mama is holding a cup, that Mama is holding that thing that contains milk or juice and for some reason she is saying *cup*. Curiously, Mama wants baby to *see* the cup. "See the cup," Mama says and baby is wondering, "What does she mean *see?*" then "What do I mean *mean?*" Blah blah, blah blah, blah blah blah blah. So, here I am trying to illustrate something, trying to articulate something to myself, with no expertise or real knowledge, de facto or otherwise, or any right to suggest or assume that I can do either, but nonetheless trying to sufficiently impact (a verb I still cannot quite accept) your judgment so that you might imagine at least that there is some thing in this world to which I would like you to attend.

* * *

His skin is pink, his nails yellowed and hard and grooved crosswise, his knuckles hairy, some of them, his skin pink and cracked, dry, chapped patterns formed in the creases between his thumbs and forefingers, as if ready to split, bleed, or fold open from itself to reveal the pink meat within, and as I stretch the silver duct tape taut then lay it against that skin, the skin of his knobbed wrists, crossed one over the other, I can see the yellow hairs seeming to rise to meet the adhesive, the ripping sound of the tape peeling from itself filling the room, then ceasing, leaving the silence clean enough to find the small sounds of this finite world, the sound of my own heart, surprisingly slow and steady, the sound of my breathing, a slight rattle in my chest, and of his breathing, clearer than my own, but rapid and short and small, and then the sound of one of his nervous yellowed nails scratching at the fir plank against which he is tied, the blond wood giving up a worm of a sliver that crawls under his nail into his flesh, and I imagine that the pain is reconnecting him with the world, and so I yank off another length of tape and let the noise hang in the air so that I can again have his senses, so that I am controlling what he senses, his hearing the tape and forgetting the splinter, and he must wonder about the subsequent silence and wonder where this length of tape will go, and he must wonder about the spectacle of it all, only the two of us alone in this place, but maybe not only us, perhaps a room full of silent spectators, because he cannot know whether others have been summoned to observe, whether he is in fact in a public square of sorts, where people will see with their own eyes so that they might be made afraid or made whole, whether they are exercising their right to be witnesses, because a hidden execution is a privileged execution and the fear of people is always that it might not happen with appropriate severity, that it might not happen at all, but he probably isn't concerned with all that now as his finger along with rest of his pink flesh becomes number and pinker, as his lips chap and dry before my eyes, the corners of his mouth becoming crustier and whiter, and I see that the edge of the tape that covers his eyes is coming undone because of his sweat and that is where I put the freshly torn strip, feeling as I do what might be a sigh of relief as he finally knows where the tape is going, and so I rip off another long, loud tear, stick it to the wall behind, and then I rip off another, and I watch his forehead wrinkle above the edge of the tape, and as I examine the edge of it, a couple of threads fraying white from its silver, I think of my assertion that he is guilty and of his claim that he is innocent, and I consider what makes any statement true, taking into account the factors of meaning and fact, taking into account lies and fictions, taking into account that no one gives a rat's ass anyway, but I entertain it all nonetheless, knowing that expecting my meaning to match the facts as a standard of truth rings of some kind of correspondence theory of truth and of course that is just a shallow grave of a theory, the fact remaining that I am tearing off strip after strip of my 3M duct tape like music in this damp room that is my basement, that is my world, that is my dark corner and passage to light and sweet bedcovers and the cold pit that is my stomach, my daughter's voice speaking to me but saying nothing, but reminding me that she once was, that I did not dream her, that her voice was attached to a vessel, a vessel that was her body, sweet and brown and not pink like this one tied to my fir plank in my sweet basement where the music is not my baby's voice, but strip torn after strip torn and strip torn after strip torn . . . the music of my torture, learned well from my world, my culture, my government, my hand searching for trembling, but not finding any anxious movement, steady as a rock, cool as a cucumber, a chill running up my spine, not raising a hair, but settling like comfort, like sweet breath against my skin, my brown skin, my dark skin, my unpink skin, while strip after strip of silver tape hang stuck to the wall, quarter notes on a staff, rest measures, and then the house settles, as houses settle and creaks with the weight of gravity, and we both, I and my subject, I will call him my subject, must be glad because at least gravity has not abandoned us to some other reality, at least gravity still pulls the same way, at least gravity is predictable and therefore ours, and I imagine what gravity is saying to him, tied to that plank, the poor bastard, listening to gravity like a fool listens to his fool of a friend, like the hawks listen to the seasons that can no longer be trusted, perched in high branches and wondering why life moves so slowly and strangely down below, when it does move.

***

Lastly, imaghost sublimighty.

Allways imessgine the weaves at the breach.

Now pushking, rearing, constant, undenifable.

Ever may you may luke at the seind and at the soon.

Imassing a storm.

Severely imagure the surf.

Deadly huge, rollackng, massive, sowell after swell, thundjurious.

Ever still you kinknot terror your eyes aweee.

And you killnow that the wives will newt reach you.

Duely the waves are furightning and though you are not afreud, you fear these waves.

Do you understand me?

***

My life before leaving Charlotte is left to me in wrinkled snapshots of good times: her smile when I would meet her at the door, her silly running through the house with her arms unmoving by her sides, her face smeared with dirt from the garden; and all the those pictures came to me with sadness and pain as I could only imagine that I had taken those things away from her. She changed after I left, much as I had changed before I left. She was sullen and quiet, but never weak and I suppose, in some way, I wish she had become weak because I loved her strength and it would have helped if I didn't love her anymore, could have found a way to not love her anymore. But I did love her, in that way no one ever wants to hear about, in that way that only seems patronizing and hollow like a platitude. I often wanted her to know how much I ached, hurt, how much I did miss her, but it was a selfish desire, my hoping that her hurt would be diminished, not so much as a relief to her, but as some kind of salve for my guilt.

***

Answer to puzzle: Kill the monster.

***

Me wlife pryor to leavening Charm's Lot is lift zen snoop-shits of vetter thymes, her miles when I whood me eat here at the dour, her shrilly runing thorough the whouse, hurt farce seam-eared with dirth from the god's den . . .

***

Don't quine for me, Argentina.

Science might in fact be the redemption of language.

The language in which we are speaking is his before it is mine.

***

There once was a lad with congenital analgesia
Who couldn't have felt the pains that could kill ya.
Inside things did grow.
Of them he could not know.
So he was buried in a bed of camellias.

Would that that limerick was about you. Oh, the smell of camellias. They don't do well here. But then neither do you. My fingers have been itching lately and I can't stop it. I try not to scratch, but I can't help it. What about your itches? Do you still have them? Your itches. Can you reach them? Do they still reach you?

***

I may not be at fault or to blame, but I am guilty for the death of my child. Though I did not ever intend her harm, though I did not ever place her in harm's way, though I was ignorant to the circumstances of the harm that came to her, I was and am guilty for I am answerable for the entirety of my actions and the totality of the actions of my world, tragic conflicts aside, explanations and excuses of madness and delusion and distraction and absence aside, I am guilty and no one can take that from me, for my guilt will make me a hero, my guilt will make all things right in my world, and for all the wrong and injury that comes to anyone in the world I touch I will be guilty also. My guilt, sick as it is, is mine and I admit this, for it allows so much room for satisfying action, for it is selfish and indulgent and I will enjoy it, for my world is crushed enough that I must enjoy something. My guilt emanates from my feeling soul, my greedy, personal, selfish, annoyingly loud feeling soul, the domain of instinct, innate motive, from nature and in nature there is no mercy, no compassion or lenity, no pity, only luck. Guilt is not an indifferent, abstracted, ambiguous affair.

* * *

Sally leaned back in her chair and looked every bit the wizened old editor, though she was only fifty and an agent. She pushed my manuscript toward me on her desk and said, "This is good. This will sell. Tell me, is it what you want to write?"

"The title is *The Wind's Kiss*," I said. "Of course this isn't what I want to write. I wrote this to make money."

"And you will. You do this very well."

"I know. It upsets me no end. I hate even reading it. I of course can't use my real name."

"Of course you can't. Or your real face. I've never seen a face so poorly suited for this genre. And another thing, just for the record, I've been around for a while, and I've never met anyone who could write this kind of book without liking it."

"Now you have."

"It's a great title."

"I've been thinking about this mission of art. I don't believe that art is supposed to stand there like an open door or gate. It's supposed to be a wall, a wall that has to be scaled or a minefield that has to be negotiated."

"Where is this coming from? What you talking about?" She lit a cigarette and stared at me.

"My art."

"Are you all right?"

"Yes."

"Fuck art. Who are you kidding? You don't make art. You're going to be rich."

"I'd rather be happy."

"Shut up and settle for rich."

***

I have glued his hand to his hand and both hands to the board. I have used super glue, in particular a product called Crazy Glue, in a ridiculously little tube that is supposed to suggest potency, sort of the opposite of male penis-size lore, and it has worked and I wonder how it has worked, how it does work. There are many theories and they all comfort me, the science of them, the coldness of them, the distance they allow me and the closeness they give me to my singular context. The simplest is the mechanical-interlock theory, based on the idea that at the microscopic level all surfaces are rough, made up of pores and bumps and ridges, and so the adhesive penetrates these spaces and forms a strong surface bond. The weakness of the adhesive itself is the weakness of the bond. Then there is the theory that the adhesive changes the surface of the adherent, the adhesive spreads when the join is formed. The resultant adhesive materials developed with this as the underlying understanding of adhesion have a lower surface tension than the adherent surfaces. During the event of contact between the adhesive and the adherent, the adhesive strength arises as a result of secondary intermolecular forces at the interface—dipole-dipole, dipole-induced dipole interactions, hydrogen bonds. A variation of this theory holds that stronger bonds form across the joint interface. The introduction of molecular bonding between adhesive and the adherents will improve the adhesive-bond strength, this being achieved by reactions at the surfaces, using surface treatments or coupling agents. If I pull his hands away from the fir with sufficient force, his flesh will be ripped from his body and I wonder if that is a good bond or a bad bond because I am trying to bond him to the board and not merely his flesh. There is the electrostatic theory, my favorite, holding that an electostatically charged double bond forms at the bond surface as a result of the interaction of the adhesive and the adherent. Apparently, many doubt the actual significance of the forces involved, claiming that no changes in adhesion performance result with gross variation in the electronic character of adhesives. I like it because no one else does, and so adhesion feels like a mystery of sorts. Then there is the diffusion theory. When an adhesive contains an adherent solvent, the adhesive can diffuse into the adherent substrate with and interchange of molecules. I suppose this is not unlike a molecular interlock–enabled adhesion. And then there is the weak-boundary-layer theory, which is the scariest because of the obvious metaphoric implications, and it holds that there are surface layers for both the adhesive and the adherents, and that these layers are ideally removed by surface treatments, and that the adherents and the adhesive are more or less alike and bond because they are in some way the same thing.

***

"Shan't!" said the cook.

***

Timaeus presents the deformation of the booty of the swirl and then of the whorl soul. The worldywooly is a slaving critter, an animule, compressed of sody and bole. That on witch the oneniverse is pitterpatterned kintains every insayible thing; the oneniverse consosquintly shoed be an andymale that containts evry ken of andymale. The bawdy of the whorlyglobe is composted of fear, air, earth, und vater, proportended to one the other. The wigglyround exhoists these fore, they are entirely wellthin it, and so hit is theairby incapistal of chaining as a hole. The primacy of the good. The finalcy of the brood. The penalsy of the hood.

* * *

Lane was pressing Play-Doh through an extruder. I sat next to her and asked her what she was making.

"The future," she said. Her small hand worked the plastic crank. "The future."

I looked at the long, red, star-shaped snake. "The future. Is this the future?"

"Yes."

"How does this represent the future?" I asked. I touched the snake and then put my fingers to my nose to smell the Play-Doh. I looked at her and waited for an answer.

Her six-year-old face twisted slightly at my question. "It doesn't present the future. It is the future."

* * *

Deep in the velveteen darkness there is movement, and I am sure it is not animal movement, and there is no worse movement in the woods than human movement, and there it is, in the brush, in the deep darkness, down the slope from the dam where I lie with my shotgun, a weapon that has been bored to full choke, and so my chances of missing are increased, but also are my chances for doing significant harm. My shotgun is old, a Winchester Model 12 with ventilated rib. It came with the house. It is loaded, here in the dark, no moon, only sneaking sounds in the brush below me, with one and one-eighth loads of number 8 shot, each containing 460 pellets. It is a cold weapon, but each time I lift it, feel its weight, I feel so, so, so American, with my full choke bore and so many chances to miss and so much potential to do harm, so American, I might fire into the night just to see the flash of the barrel, to have my ears ring, and scare most of the world that are these woods and kill something, someone, something. *But wait! What would Jesus do? Jesus would turn the water into wine and get them drunk and together they would make a wildlife film, with bears and crows and newts and then when they weren't looking, when the dope-selling, fiancée-beating scumbags weren't looking, Jesus would have the bears eat them limb from limb and the crows peck out their evil eyes and the newts would do whatever it is that newts do and there would be awful screaming and Jesus would turn the wine back into water and find somebody to have divine sex with. That's what Jesus would do and all of this is here because I can put it here and it's here to piss off any Jesus-lovers that might happen upon this and even though I don't have anything against Jesus-lovers, they apparently have something against me, as does, probably, Jesus or his scumbag daddy in white silk boxing trunks.* I am in velveteen, like I said, darkness, a cocoon of sweet lightless nothingness, and yet there is something in the dark wood below me. And then I realize that I don't want to shoot anyone, that this water simply is not all that important, that our game of diverting the water back and forth, left and right, is fun enough, could even be a way of life, but I really don't like this gun. The men-creatures below in the thicket mean me no harm. I am not a bad man. I don't want to hurt them, to kill them. I don't even want to scare them, really. So, I take my weapon by its cold barrel and my blanket and myself up along the creek side, up away from the dam and in the darkness there, I watch, almost peacefully, while the pot growers begin to alter the flow of the water to nature's intended path. Somehow my covert observation of them is killing enough, I think, for a moment. After they leave, I will go down and reverse their efforts immediately. This is our game. But games have rules only because they can be broken, and I haven't told them the rules anyway, and they don't give a damn about me or my garden or Jesus or the little girl who will get killed by their drugs, and suddenly my shotgun feels warmer. The night feels warmer. The floodgates of rage and anger and justice and the AMERICAN WAY open and it all, all of it, becomes water again, water under the bridge pounding, pounding, pounding on the stanchions, the understructure, the underpinnings, sloshing against the blocks and legs and foundation of everything that Jesus and I hold sacred. Right, Jessie? So, bang bang away. Bang.

***

So, in my novel A does this and B responds thusly and causes C to become upset with A and B believes that A knew all along that C would become upset and was in fact counting on it and so B hates A but also is greatly disappointed that C has behaved so predictably and C becomes offended that B is arrogant enough to stand in judgment and sleeps with A though neither A nor C have feelings for each other and A discovers midcoitus that B is the real object of C's desire and B wanders in to find A and C in the compromised pose and in a fit of madness cuts himself in half and become two little D's that run around and around looking to get the F out of there, crying "EEEEEEEEEE" all the while.

***

Looking at the broken edge of the part is one of the first steps in metal identification for the welding operator engaged in repair and maintenance work. When looking at the fractured surface, he observes such things as the nature of the break, the type of grain, and the color of the grain. The surface of a fracture on a piece of gray cast iron is dark gray and usually will rub off black on the fingertip. White cast iron has a very bright silvery appearance.

Looming Atabrine theater brolly edh ofay theater partake isallobar oneiric ofay theater firth stephanotis inability metalanguage ideogram fora theater welfare opercular engerlanded inability repand andalusite maintop world. Whenas . . . appease.

Everything is one step removed.

***

There is a fall, she said, my wife, there is a fall and you have lived it and you have seen it and I have seen it, she said, there is a fall from good, from grace maybe, and I have seen you and what you are and what you have become. Are you happy now?

she asked. Are you happy now that you have broken me into little pieces, undone all those words that you put in my ear, undone all the love I gave you? There is a fall and you have felt it and I have seen it and you have let me down and I hope you will hurt forever.

    —Lane is upstreamstairs gettingerah hert tootooth-bristling. Where hearth you gowing?

    —We're going to derive up the coastward and static at that weired lewdking palace, the Madonna Inn. She's hallways commented on it, comme il faut.

    —Yeah.

    —How argot you do in?

    —I'm gyrate. A look beak achristen the room, tellward the beckettshelves perhaps. I've bent raiding a loot. I'll see a cripple of movings this weakened.

    —That zounds fume.

    —Lane, honin, furry it up!

    —Sly poke.

    —Alweighs.

    —You look will, Charlotte. You leak good.

    Lane is tall feet on the starings.

    —Hair you are. Live me a kiss. You save a goose timbre know.

***

Why will I bury you?
So that one day I might disturb your grave.

***

"Yes," I said to the detective, "that's my daughter. She's all there." I didn't know why I added that, except that somewhere in my mind I imagined the police still out there looking for some piece of her. I was no doubt saying it to myself so that I would in fact stop searching. But of course I wouldn't; I would scan the eyes of every child I would meet, seeking some bit of my little girl. Her eyes were closed and I recalled photographs I had seen of dead children from the early twentieth century, their peaceful faces made somehow more peaceful by the placement of pennies on their eyes to keep them closed or, as I learned later, to pay the ferryman. I wanted to reach out and touch my daughter, but I couldn't bring myself to do it, and they would not have let me anyway. She was so far away there on that metal slab. The examiner was decent enough to not slide her back into the refrigerated wall while I was watching, but I heard the sound of the drawer's return as I exited the room, the detective's hand placed consolingly, oddly, against the small of my back.

* * *

I am sharpening knives and I am imagining, trying to imagine, that things at any point can remain the same, unchanged, static, and the thought or the possibility of the thought (as it is a thought I'm not sure I have actually achieved) is making my head spin. For one, I am trying to imagine a state where *things* do not change and I don't know, in the first place, what *things* means. Define your terms, they taught us in school and then the teacher would look out the window and say *it* was raining. What is raining? The cranky baby inside my head would ask.

Define the *it!* A tired old silly question. But I am sharpening my knives on my grinder, and with every electric spin something is changed, the blade of the knife is more honed or less depending on the angle, the static field between me and the wheel has altered in electromagnetic intensity, there is wear on the bearings of the grinder's motor, the amount of pressure my fingers exert against the blade shifts, my levels of exhilaration and disappointment rise and fall in turns, and the pressure of my mere observation, quantum physics tells me, affects the process itself. I recall cartoons where single strands of hair were floated over and then sliced by swords to check sharpness, but my hairs are short and curly and will not be easily laid over a blade. I will have to use something else.

***

These are the sounds of my footsteps.

***

No I text am contains here in to it torture its this own man context. Context this is man always killed external my to child the and thing dreams said. How can you I are continue to breathe understand while a he text is is never alive there in in the this text world.

***

"I was at the market with a basket of eggs and a fat man stepped on it while I was tying my sneaker. The fat man offered to pay for my eggs and asked how many I had bought, but I couldn't recall the exact number. When I took them out two at a time, there was one egg left. And so it was when I pulled them out three at a time and four at a time and five and six at a time. But when I pulled the eggs out seven at a time, they came out even. What is the smallest number of eggs I could have had?"

"I don't understand."

"It's a problem," I said. "Solve it and I will not hurt you."

"Please."

"You could have asked my Lane such a riddle and given her a chance to win her life. Perhaps you did. Did you pose a riddle to my little girl?"

"Please."

"I'm sure you didn't. What if I give you another problem?"

"Please."

"Perhaps numbers are too difficult. What about this? What is the longest word? Well? Too slow. *Smiles.* There is a mile between the two s's. Lane loved that one. Does that hurt?"

"Please."

"Have you ever been bitten?" I asked and he just looked at me. "I know that you have. My daughter bit you. Is that too tight? Of course it is. She bit you. The forensic odontologist found bites on your arm. My little girl had a slight overbite. You probably didn't know that. A malocclusion, very slight. She was going to have braces in six months. Did it hurt when she bit you?"

"I'm sorry."

"Let me read this to you. 'Coroner's Inspector arrived scene at 7:10 a.m. Exterior temperature: 48 degrees F/8.8 degrees C. Relative humidity: 65 percent.

"'Coroner was directed down an east-facing slope to a ditch and observed a lifeless human body under a small shrub, a child between eight and twelve. The body was facing the bottom of the ditch. There were white sneakers on her feet and the rest of the body was naked. Coroner verified that the victim had no signs of life and pronounced the victim dead at 7:18.

"'Coroner noted bruising on the upper neck of the victim and bruises on the upper arms and shoulders. The victim's right arm was twisted at a severe angle behind the back and appeared to be broken. Rigor mortis was well established throughout the body. Liver temperature at the scene was 87 degrees F/ 30.6 degrees C. Skin was waxy and cool to the touch. Eyes were open and the corneas were clouded. The sclerae were clear. There was trauma to the vagina and there was evidence of bleeding from the vagina consistent with sexual penetration. There was extensive bruising on the upper thighs and near the anus. Preliminary estimate for time of death: ten to twelve hours prior to examination. Preliminary finding is for sexual battery. Apparent cause of death: strangulation. Body removed from scene at 8:00 a.m.'"

***

***

It is five o'clock in the morning. I am going about my morning chores. They are the same every morning and so I am not really awake, but moving through the so-well-known actions, each done as if according to some rule, each done as if a preliminary to some game that I have played a thousand times, but it is preliminary so it takes nothing of my mind, like setting up the board for chess or rigging the net for badminton.

I am cleaning and straightening and making breakfast and preparing my desk for another day that will see no writing. If I had a Bible I would read it, and I imagine that somehow it would give me comfort if I were stupid, and some questions if I were curious, but would give nothing else no matter how I might be. If I had a big wooden cross I would burn it, and the heat of the flame would give me peace, as I'm certain it has for so many others. I have a garden, so I water it. And there is my flycatcher friend, muted yet brilliant and sweet rust and in the wrong place.

A fat man and his wife have taken the wrong turn down the mountain and have driven into my yard. I tell them they are in the wrong place. They tell me that my place is beautiful. I tell them that they really are in the wrong place. What I say is,

"You're really in the wrong place."

The fat man wipes sweat from his face and neck with a much-used patterned handkerchief and looks at my house. "Wow, you live way up, don't you?"

His wife tugs on his arm. "He wants us to go."

"Are you famous?" The fat man looks at me, then back at my house.

"Not yet," I say, and I look at his wife's eyes.

"Come on." She says his name, but I can't make it out, though I imagine it has one syllable.

He senses that she is frightened and loads himself back behind the wheel. I can see him checking me out in his mirror as they roll away. I don't wave.

Initially, I adopted a pseudonymous existence both as a means and as an end. A black man wasn't going to sell many romance novels to school middle-aged perm-headed naildecaled bus drivers, beauticians, and trailer parkers. I also enjoyed my anonymity for its own sake to some extent. And it served some kind of Zen region of my soul by feeding my lack of ambition or desire for fame and attention, a lack for which I felt great and notably ironic pride.

And as the car rounded the bend I replayed my response to the fat man's question about my fame. "Not yet." Not yet.

***

. . . and of the three lives, the three heads, the three, not four, not two, but three, could there ever have been any befuddlement over whether the center was centered, whether one was in the middle, a focal point, a vocal point, within the crosshairs, a targeted blight in the three-treed forest of blights, the big puppy of the litter, the red dot within two red circles all separated by white, the color of snow, the color of foam on forgotten beaches, the color of clouds and china and funny that it used to be called bone china or how it was ever called china at all and funny how people can stand so close to it when it breaks and funny how people can stand so close to the killing and still find a way to breathe, how people can go to shows and movies and games where grown men jump high to slam a ball through a hole and to dinner where they gaze out the window at the suffering in the rain-glistening and oil-slick-sick street, at the staggering waste in the gutters, at limbs that twist in the wind, that gnarl in the sun, that break and heal and break and heal without ever being set, set in the middle as if apart from the other two, thieves in the night, strapped to the ever-present plank, still wet, wet with, wet from, discolored by, white so easily discolored, the spots showing up in the light, the light of day, the light of dawning, the light of recognition as the gurgling becomes louder, the drowning becomes concrete, of all things concrete, the fear recedes into, well, recognition and here we are again, recognizing the recognized, acknowledging the acknowledged, knowing the known, fucking the fucked and killing the dead while somewhere a band with seventy-six American white-bread red-blooded eagle-beaked trombones leading the way is performing for some we-call-them-troops, support-the-troops, decent-American-boys in some sandy faraway, some sand-gusty pit while they jackknife blood from beneath their nails, enjoying the coronets and clarinets and marionettes and raisinettes and raisons d'être in million-degree sunshine and thousand-fold guilt because they know they could have said no, should have said no, as I know I could have said no, should have said no, but didn't say no and I wouldn't say no, whether it is no matter or know matter or whether it matters to know to say no, but of course I didn't say no and that is what I must sleep and wake with each and every morning of my miserable, pathetic, brokenhearted, tormented, woebegone, dolorous and long, long, long, long life and notice that I did not write *tragic,* because with that word might live, could live, perchance live an iota of dignity and that, especially that, is something I will not understand . . .

***

During the summers Lane would come with me to fish. We would awake early, make the drive down the mountain, and drive north toward Questa. She would always want to stop and have breakfast at the little diner there that catered to bandana-headed bikers. The waitress was a mini-skirted, young woman who loved my daughter. She'd call her "squirt" and always get a smile. "What'll it be, squirt?" "Who's this you dragged in with you today, squirt?"

"Where's squirt?" the woman asked me, just months after Lane's death.

"My daughter died," I told her, rather flatly. I watched her as she found nothing to say, but stared at me, wanting to offer me something, anything. "There's not much to say," I said, then added, "She always liked you."

"I'm so sorry," she said.

"Thank you. I'll have the chili."

"I'm so sorry."

I found myself staring at her apron. It was gingham, and even then I was not attending to the color, but to the squares, each so defined and individual and yet without all of them there would have been no pattern, or at least the pattern would not have been what it was. Each of the identical squares was necessary for the monotonous truth of the object itself. Each square was any other square was any other square was any other square. It was dark out, and a car made a sound on the rain-slick highway.

I ate my chili with beans. Then I heard the cook say he was done and leaving, and then it was the only waitress there with me, just the two of us on the wet highway in Questa.

She came back to fill my water glass. "Are you going to be needing anything else?"

"I'm good."

She paused to look out at the road. Headlights flashed by. I put my hand on her leg, behind her knee, and as I did this I realized that she was an attractive woman, but not very attractive, and then I wondered what that had to do with anything. She didn't move as I placed my palm flat against the back of her thigh. Her skin there was soft but not very smooth.

"You were in here a few months ago," she said. "I remember. It was cold."

"I'm sorry," I said, pulling my hand back to the table. I played with the spoon.

"You have a place around here?" she asked.

I nodded.

"I live in Red River."

"I shouldn't have done that," I said. I put my napkin on the table. "I apologize."

"We all get lonely." She seemed to lean away, looking out the window, but she didn't really seem any farther from me. "I have to clean up here. I get left to do all the cleaning on Mondays. It's such a quiet day and night. There's never much to clean, at least."

"I'm finished. I don't want to hold you up."

She laughed at that. "Hold me up," she said.

"Poor choice of words." I put money down on the table. "You've been very kind."

"You bet."

I looked at her eyes. They were blue and tired. She had a washed-out look, the look of a poor mother. For whatever reason, probably pity, I knew that if I pressed the situation, she would take me home, have sex with me. The thought was a bad one, but somehow the mere possibility of her openness, her sharing of her own personal and singular desperation, was genuine and so kind.

"Come again," she said as I walked to the door. "Thank you."

***

Sai sai whathut you light, but Zeno ist the farther of calqueuelust. Thehair is noting newt neath the sund livenits nutswitstooding.

***

We, all of us, are just and always points and lines. Rolle on big river. A circle is just a straight line that is at every point equidistant from one point. Oh, home on lagrange. A quadrangle is four lines intersecting in space. The point has no dimensions, is merely location. The line has no depth, is merely direction, and space is nothing. Move forward with cauchyson.

***

Ishmael, I can't find her. She was here, and then she wasn't. I can't find her. I can't find her. I checked the neighbors, and they haven't seen her.

I'm sure she's around.

She was on her bicycle, and then when I looked out the window, she wasn't there. She never leaves her bike on the street. She never has before.

She probably chased after a stray dog or cat. You know how she is when she sees an animal. I'm coming over.

She never leaves her bike there, not there, not by the street like that. She loves that bicycle. I drove around the block, the next block, and through the little alley.

Call the police.

The police? Ishmael, I'm scared.

I'll be right over.

***

Then, suddenly, as if the idea had never occurred to me, but of course it had, many times, nightly even, but still suddenly, as if the idea could move with only one speed, knew only one speed, a full gallop, it came knocking knocking knocking, a notion all too familiar, and jarring perhaps for that fact of that familiarity, the idea that I could make things, if not right, then somehow more true to the order of all other things, more righteous maybe, though what a word worthy of disdain, or perhaps I knew that I could merely distend and magnify the tangle and observe that chaos is finally the order that would have this world, any world for that matter, make some kind of sense to me. Blood on my hands. Who, in his or anyone else's right mind, would want the stain removed? Suddenly.

And isn't it the nature of blood to stick to things? Abstract things and concrete things. Real things and imagined things. Those we love and those we hate. Blood is not bad, it just is. And blood will have blood.

***

As if anything matters?

***

Sally wandered, pigeon-toed and sock-footed, close to the hollow wooden door that led down to the basement. I watched her from where I stood in the kitchen chopping carrots and apples for the salad. She studied the door. She felt or heard something, I could see that by the way she cocked her head. Her face appeared so much younger in that moment, the whiskey and smoke at the corners of her eyes clearly, ever so briefly.

"What's down there?" she asked. And even her voice seemed younger.

"Nothing," I said. "Nothing but basement stuff. Dust and bugs and the like."

"I hear something."

"Sounds," I said. "A house breathes. Often I think that dust makes a house cough."

She stared at the door. Her hand didn't move from her side, but I could imagine its trajectory to the knob.

"I wouldn't open that," I said.

"Bugs?"

I nodded.

She joined me at the counter and began to put leaves into the spinner. "I hate bugs."

"Most of us do."

***

What is this business about shadows and cave walls and a big fire? Are the brownies almost done?

> Plato: So, you get the picture of the cave and big fire?
> Glaucon: I do.
> Plato: And can you see the men walking by, carrying
> things?
> Glaucon: I do.

Plato: Some carrying vessels, some carrying wood, some talking.

Glaucon: I do.

Plato: Can you see that they see only their shadows on the wall?

Glaucon: I do.

Plato: And only the shadows of the objects they carry?

Glaucon: I do.

Plato: And if they were to talk, wouldn't they name the things before them?

Glaucon: They would.

Plato: But remember that all they see is shadows, and further suppose that an echo circles round, comes from the other side of the camp, and that they cannot see where it comes from, that in fact they hear only the echo and not the voice, and, really, I want you to imagine now that all these men see is the mere shadows of images and nothing at all more, and I want you to tell me just what it is then that they are naming.

Glaucon: May we eat now?

***

and it's like this, like this, Reggie, W., nameless one, I am neither impressed nor stirred by the fact that you are afraid of me, that does nothing for me, fills no gaps, soothes no wounds, as what I want is for you to find me fearful, and I know that this is hard for you to grasp, to get your small tortured brain around, though I am certain that on some level you are capable of some sort of understanding, even if you will never be able to articulate it, but there is nothing for me to do as I drive you back along this same highway, letting the same cacti mark the passing of time and distance, except to explain, whether my attempt is vain or not, the nature of the sublime or, perhaps more correctly put, the sublime in nature, and you may choose to listen or not, but you will hear and you will hear that what I want to be, am, will be is sublime in your eyes, even if you don't know it or comprehend what in the fuck I'm talking about, and I want you to take time and with your mind review, go over, take an inventory of your body, realize that there are no, external anyway, parts missing, you are bleeding from no place, you bear no bruises or other marks, realize, in other words, that I have left no sign, no sign of my presence, no sign of our connection, no sign of my art, my business with you, realize that you don't know who I am, don't know where you've been, don't know anything, but you do have a vague recollection, one from long ago, on a cool night, of my face, faint, vague, and ghostly, mere suggestion, like the face of god, except of course that I exist, maybe, and I don't want you to fear me, not in some crass childish cowardly way, because a man who fears in that way is incapable of truly realizing, comprehending the sublime in nature, just as the man who is a slave to inclination and appetite can have no true appreciation, recognition of beauty, and I say this, trying to make it clear that I don't desire for you ever to take flight at the sight, sound, or thought of me, but rather to stand in absolute awe, to then take a step back and dispassionately, soberly, even serenely assess my fury, my power, my might, and I want you to find a perverse and uneasy satisfaction, a strange comfort, in your state of terror, a state that should approximate joy, but not quite, as I almost want you to find peace in the knowledge of my existence, in the knowledge that if I found you once I will find you again, almost, almost peace, as I want the terror in your heart to remain pure, I want the terror to wake you in the morning and sleep with you at night and remind you of the fragility of life, of the thinness of forgiveness and absolution, and I want you to pray to me, pray that I don't come back and that I never leave you, pray that my might is distant and my countenance somehow sated, pray daily, my friend, and perhaps that will keep me at bay and remember, know that I have killed, will kill, and that is only part of what instills fear, that what chills your blood is the fact that I can give life, that it is my gift to give . . .

***

***

Howl miny linends befear we scar what wee are? Howl manly steeroakes afore a think is what tis? And leven thin, is it that thering or mere represistation?

***

Je ne dis pas cela, mais enfin lui disais-je . . .

***

Gnarly the nixt mourning, a defective, a wombman, keyme to Carelot's dour and we call thaw this as a bid sighn and din pact twas, as the mews she deviled was that a jung guirrel matchking Lane's dyscryption had beleaf sound kin a ravene bedsighed a parque by twooth bouys and fir daweg. Ze deflec-tif aid gone intel soul mud detale that it screamed tome abit the parque, tit leaiding to a dwitch that fled into a consecrete brainage carnail, and the beyes, daged nilne and tend, knot bothers, but hacriss-the-strait gnawhboys, that I found my-self asking, without knowing why or even that I was asking, "What kind of dog was it?"

***

Mirror set by mirror facing mirror showing mirror reflecting mirror etching mirror casting mirror back and forth and forth and back with his face at one end, but where? with his face at one end and mirror upon mirror, taking no energy to work, making reflections that have no end, no other end, just infinite middle, infinite faces that are not his, for him to see, his rough face made smooth, his head halved in size by distance again and again, gaze and return, and not a single photon his, and his guilty eyes well up and who cares if the tears or the guilt are true? and there they stand and hang, mirrors all, windows all, my guilt as shameless as it is sincere, my killing as real as it is passionate, my tears as phony as my dear land's promises, thwack, whack, slash, I am a good citizen, patrolling my own borders and keeping my own peace and nailing my own mirrors into place even if they are set to cast no reflections of my own and Sally and Bucky and Art and Charlotte and Charley and the dead dealers and the woman at the roadside diner populate my dreams as if my dreams are mine, were ever mine, and the little flycatcher, her color muted and tasteful, darts about or lights nearby and I know her, have known her, must know her, her familiar voice a bridge to my past, a bridge over all this blood, nights of cleaning blood, wiping blood, scrubbing blood, finding blood on sofa pillows, on books in the case, on the spine of *The Way of All Flesh,* on the pages of *Ulysses,* on the unsharpened ends of pencils, on the sweater I never wear, dried black in places so no one would guess that it is blood and not my blood because I have managed to keep all of my blood in its bottle, filled to the top against its cap, pressing up into its cap and making me hurt in my cap while I recall the last breath of the last life that I stole, rightly, righteously, correctly, justifiedly, honorably, sinlessly, done with precision and calm, always calm, a true indicator of the rightness of any action, because someone always has to pay, shoot the ocean if it rises too high, stab the wind if it blows too hard, strangle the night if it falls too dark, but punish someone, something, someplace, somehow, and confess without apology and confess without concern and confess because my confession is an admission of righteousness, but hide what I have done, because the night will never fall dark enough, because the little flycatcher doesn't care about my guilt or innocence, only about the blood that stains my nails the color of her feathers, but with no purity of light, lightness of flight, weightless in the light of day, caring nothing about the questions I ask only to find the answers I need, but then there are the other questions: *Will my daughter grow older in my dreams? Why do reasonable people entertain the ontological argument?* and *What kind of dog was it?* And the answers are: *No, Because they can,* and *Some kind of retriever.*

Percival Everett is a Distinguished Professor of English at the University of Southern California and the author of twenty books, including *Wounded, Erasure,* and *Glyph*. He lives in Los Angeles.

The text of *The Water Cure* is set in Adobe Caslon Pro, a typeface by Carol Twombly based on eighteenth-century type designs by William Caslon. This book was designed by Ann Sudmeier. Composition at Prism Publishing Center. Manufactured by Sheridan Books on acid-free paper.